Zoey clamped a pillow over her head. She felt sick. Her hands were trembling. Her skin felt crawly. Her legs were drawn up to her chest in a fetal position. She wanted to throw up, but she couldn't move, and still violent words tore through walls and pillows and all her pitiful defenses to rip at her heart.

It was happening. It was happening right now, without warning. Like the shattering of an atom, releasing the forces of fire and wind and poison, her family was being shattered. She could do nothing to stop it.

A slammed door, rattling the windows. And then a shriek, right at her own door. Her mother's voice, like no voice Zoey had ever heard before.

"Are you happy now, Zoey?" Her mother pounded her fist on the door to Zoey's room. "Are you happy with what you've done?"

Don't Miss Any of the Installments in

MAKING OUT

by Katherine Applegate

from Avon Flare

#1 Zoey Fools Around
#2 Jake Finds Out
#3 Nina Won't Tell
#4 Ben's in Love
#5 Claire Gets Caught
#6 What Zoey Saw

Coming Soon

#7 Lucas Gets Hurt
#8 Aisha Goes Wild

MAKING OUT #6

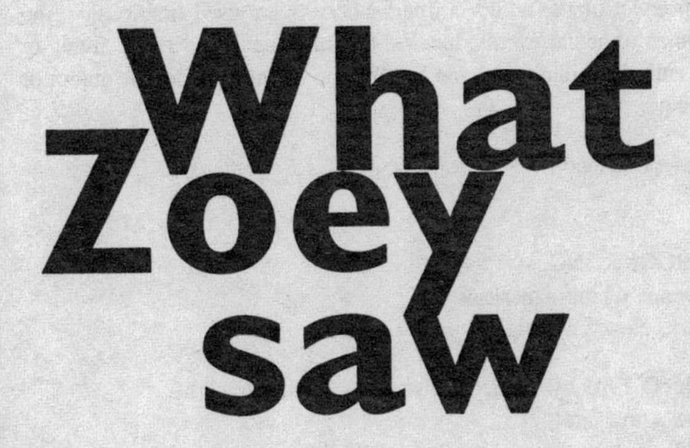

KATHERINE APPLEGATE

Originally published as *Boyfriends Girlfriends*

To Michael

Grateful acknowledgment is made for permission to reprint a quotation from *The Big Sleep* by Raymond Chandler, Vintage Knopf. Copyright © 1939 by Raymond Chandler. Reprinted by permission.

Originally published by HarperPaperbacks as *Boyfriends Girlfriends*.

AVON BOOKS, INC.
1350 Avenue of the Americas
New York, New York 10019

Published by arrangement with Daniel Weiss Associates, Inc.
Visit our website at **http://www.AvonBooks.com**
Library of Congress Catalog Card Number: 98-92791
ISBN: 0-380-80216-3

First Avon Flare Printing: November 1998

AVON FLARE TRADEMARK REG. U.S. PAT. OFF. AND IN OTHER COUNTRIES, MARCA REGISTRADA, HECHO EN U.S.A.

Printed in the U.S.A.

WCD 10 9 8 7 6 5 4 3 2 1

For my readers. Thanks.
And for Michael. Thanks again.

The bus ride took forever. Killington to Boston, then a change of buses to go to Portland and a second change to get back to Weymouth. On the ride Zoey slept a little and cried some more, hoping with what energy she could muster that Lucas would bitterly regret being such a jerk.

It was late afternoon before she caught the familiar ferry and saw the comforting silhouette of Chatham Island approaching. She was exhausted beyond belief, caught in an endless gray dream of remembered conversations, secret wishes, and resilient hopes that clung to life despite everything.

She got off the ferry and briefly considered stopping in at the restaurant. But at this time of day her father would be in the kitchen and her mother would be at home, sleeping in preparation for the Sunday night bar shift. Showing up back home a day early would just worry her father. This was more a mother-daughter type of thing.

She slogged through the streets and almost collapsed with relief on reaching her home. A good, long night of sleep and things would all seem much clearer. Maybe Lucas would call and say all the things she still desperately hoped he would say.

Maybe he had already caught the next bus and was on his way to her. Maybe.

She went in quietly, not wanting to wake her mother earlier than necessary. She dropped her bag at the foot of the stairs and made her way up.

At the top landing she heard a sound. Her mother's voice, a low murmur.

She went to her parents' bedroom door. It was open several inches.

"Mom?"

She heard a muttered curse. A rapid shuffling, another curse, this time a man's voice. A figure flashed past the open door. Running, pulling on a shirt in a frantic rush. A man.

A man, not her father.

Not her *father.*

But a man she had recognized beyond a shadow of a doubt.

Dear Zoey:

Hi, it's me, your mom. Your *mom*. It seems very strange to write that to you because right now you're not even one day old and even though I've held you a couple of times, you don't seem quite real yet. At this point in your life you weigh less than eight pounds. You're mostly bald, although the hair you do have is like gold. We don't know the color of your eyes because you haven't opened them yet. Besides, you never know with babies: your big brother Benjamin had blue eyes when he was born, but now they're brown.

I'm writing this book to you, my first little baby girl. I plan to write in it every birthday as you grow up, and then when you're sixteen I'll give it to you. You'll probably think it's lame and sentimental and be embarrassed by it, but that's tough. Someday when you're a mom with a brand-new beautiful baby girl, you'll understand.

Not that you have to be a mother when you grow up. You can be whatever you want.

As long as you're not a Republican. (Just kidding.) Or a Moonie. (Not kidding.)

Your father is right across the room now, asleep in one of the chairs. He was here during the delivery and didn't even get sick like he did when Benjamin was being born. He cried when he held you for the first time but tried not to let me see it.

I hope you like your name, by the way. We were torn between Zoey and Hillary, but Zoey sounded more laid-back.

I guess I don't know what else to say right now, and I'm

pretty tired, too. You didn't want to come out and as a result I haven't really slept in about forty-eight hours.

But I wanted to tell you right here how much your father and I wanted you, and how much we both love you. I hope we'll figure out how to be good parents to you and Benjamin. Or at least not screw up too badly.

Love,

Your mom

One

Zoey Passmore recoiled from the door, tripping backward, feeling for the door to her own room. Wave after wave of emotion, shock followed by embarrassment followed by revulsion. The silence of her room. The ringing silence of her room. Her face hot to touch, her heart pounding, her throat tight with a feeling close to panic.

The door to her mother's room had been open just a crack. Perhaps the latch hadn't caught. Perhaps *he* had been in too much of a hurry and had just been careless, swinging the door hurriedly, anxious to get on with . . .

Zoey tried to calm her breathing, sitting there on the edge of her bed, clutching the mattress with her hands, squeezing it, fingers stiff. Her chest felt constricted, as if she had to force each breath in and then couldn't exhale completely. The slanting afternoon light gave the room a grim, gray look.

Outside her room she heard a heavy tread and jumped. The sound of a large man tiptoeing down the stairs, trying far too late to be discreet. The third step squeaked and in that instant Zoey realized she hated him. Hated him and hated her mother.

If only she hadn't come home early. She should be

with her friends in Vermont now. She should never have seen any of this. She didn't want to see this. She didn't want to know.

What would her mother say to her? Would she try to lie? Would she break down in tears and swear it would never happen again? Or would she say nothing at all?

A mental image of her father working in the kitchen of the restaurant, listening to some old rock and roll while he whistled out of tune and chopped parsley or sliced onions, came vividly to Zoey's mind. While her father had been working, only a few blocks away, her mother, *his* wife . . .

The enormity of the betrayal was too much to grasp. It was inconceivable.

A light knock at her door made her start. She quickly lay back against the pillows and snatched at a nearby magazine, trembling fingers scrabbling at the slick pages. "Yes?"

"Can I come in?" Her mother, of course. Now that *he* was safely gone from the house.

"Sure," Zoey said, her voice shrill and unnatural to her own ears.

The door opened. Her mother, hair hastily pinned back, wearing jeans and a plaid shirt. Her *husband's* shirt. "What are you doing back so early?" her mother asked, looking flushed, her cheeks red, her brow damp with perspiration.

"I wasn't having much fun there," Zoey said.

Her mother nodded. Normally she would pursue the matter, but this wasn't a normal conversation. "Oh. Well . . . I was . . . I was just in my room, watching TV. I heard you come in."

"TV. Soaps, huh?" Zoey asked.

Her mother managed a half-smile. "You know how

I love my soaps. You probably heard them, you know . . .''

Yes, Zoey knew. Too bad it was Sunday afternoon and there weren't any soaps on. Too bad her mother hadn't prepared some better lie, because now Zoey could throw the truth in her face.

And then what? Tell her father? Go to him and say . . . what? I saw Mom in bed with another man, and you'll never guess who?

Instant divorce. The end of her family. The end of *her* family.

She met her mother's eyes. Her mother looked away.

''I guess I'd better take a nap,'' Zoey said. ''It was a long night.''

''Maybe later you could come down to the restaurant. We could talk about what happened on your trip.''

Zoey rolled onto her side, turning away from her mother, feeling small and ashamed. ''I don't think so.''

After a long while, Zoey heard the door close behind her.

A little over two hundred miles away and several thousand feet higher, Claire Geiger leaned into her turn and felt the edges of her skis bite, then slip. She adjusted her weight and regained her balance, accelerating as she tightened the radius of the turn.

Jake McRoyan was still ahead of her, throwing up a shower of snow, much stronger than she was. But had he read the slope correctly?

She widened her next turn, finding a patch of newly manicured snow while Jake fought his way over a small mogul field. Her way was longer but faster.

Claire glanced left, saw that she was level with, then, in a flash, ahead of him.

She crouched low to gather momentum, then crossed his path just a few feet ahead of the tips of his skis. Close enough to hear his mock-furious shout. The words were whipped away by the slipstream, but the emotion was clear enough.

Claire slowed and the two of them came to rest, panting, in the trees off the trail. She brushed snow from the front of her suit, then removed one glove to run her fingers through her glossy black hair, combing out a fallen pine needle. She laughed triumphantly.

"That's the first time you beat me today," Jake said.

"The first time I really tried."

"Ha."

"Besides, it's our last run today, so it's the one that counts," Claire said, pushing her yellow wraparound shades back on her head. The slope was falling into shadow.

"Who made up that rule?" Jake demanded.

"Me."

"Then I get to make up rules, too," Jake said. He dug in his poles and brought his skis parallel with hers so that they stood side by side. "My rule is winner has to kiss the loser."

Claire smiled. "I guess I can live with that rule."

She leaned toward him, accepting the touch of his cold lips on hers, then, as tiredness was forgotten, his much warmer tongue in her mouth. She closed her eyes, which proved to be a mistake. Her balance went, and, still clutching him, she fell over, sinking into the snow as if it were a feather bed, Jake on top of her, legs and feet hopelessly tangled in their skis.

Claire tried to get up, but now Jake held her down.

"There's no escape. We may be pinned here until help arrives," Jake said. He kissed her again.

"My entire backside's frozen," Claire observed a while later. "I can't feel my butt."

"Can I?" Jake asked, leering outrageously.

"I still have my poles," Claire pointed out, brandishing one. "And I'm prepared to use them."

Jake rolled off and levered himself upright. Then he reached down to pull Claire up. "Come on. Let's get back to the condo and grab the hot tub before anyone else does."

The tub was almost painfully hot on Claire's still-cold flesh and she had to lower herself in bit by bit, burning below the water, freezing out of it. The air around them was so cold that the water that splashed onto the wooden deck froze within minutes.

Jake was already in up to his neck, floating on churning bubbles and wreathed in steam. He was openly admiring her sheer white one-piece. *Savoring*, she decided. That was the right word.

It was still a little strange having a guy she cared for react to her that way. Strange after Benjamin, who had loved her without seeing her.

It wasn't necessarily a bad thing to have a guy think of you as more than sound and texture. Although, she realized with a certain sadness, Jake would probably never know her truer self, the thoughts and ideas and hidden motives, the way Benjamin had. Maybe no guy ever would again, because no other guy would ever be indifferent to . . . well, to the way she looked in a bathing suit.

"You're looking thoughtful," Jake remarked.

"What? You actually looked at my face?"

"Now that the rest of you's underwater, a brief glance."

Proving my point perfectly, Claire noted. Oh, well. It was naive to think that any one guy could ever be perfect in every way. And it wasn't like she didn't get a lot of pleasure from the sight of Jake's massive shoulders rising from the steaming water or from his long, corded arms stretched out around the rim of the tub.

"I was just wondering whether part of the reason Zoey left was because of the little scene you two had last night." A lie. Actually, she'd been thinking about it earlier, but she couldn't tell Jake the truth—that she had been thinking about his limitations.

A guarded look clouded his eyes. "I wondered that, too. Maybe I was too hard on her."

"I don't think you were too hard. Maybe she was just overly sensitive. After all, she *was* prying into something that's not really any of her business."

"Maybe she doesn't understand," Jake said thoughtfully. "So someone at the *Weymouth Times* heard rumors that someone on our team was using drugs. The rumor might not even be about me. I mean, it could be about some completely separate thing, right?" He looked over his shoulder self-consciously, glancing down the path in front of the deck.

"Probably all a coincidence," Claire said, pretending to agree. "I don't think she'd have agreed to write the story if she'd thought you were involved."

"Don't you?" he said eagerly. "You mean I should just tell her?"

Claire shook her head. "No. It's too late now. If

Zoey agreed to do the story, she'll most likely do it. She thinks it's integrity or something.''

Jake nodded glumly. ''Maybe she won't find out anything.''

''Are you good at keeping secrets?'' Claire asked, teasing.

''I don't know. I never had any until recently.'' Then, in a bitter voice, ''The absolute stupidest thing I have ever done in my life.''

Claire waved a hand dismissively. She was tired of this topic and wanted to luxuriate in the warmth. ''Keep quiet and it will probably all blow over,'' she advised. Then she cocked an eyebrow at him. ''Just don't try to keep secrets from me.''

It was supposed to be a throwaway line, a joke. But there had been a flicker in Jake's eyes. She formed an impish, innocent smile. ''You wouldn't ever keep secrets from me, would you?''

Jake shook his head. He looked so blatantly guilty that Claire almost pitied him.

So. Jake had something he wasn't telling her. Well, well. She could go for the kill right now, or just sit back and see how long he held out.

Jake looked around for the cold drinks he'd brought to the tub. Spotting them on the deck, he stood up, turned, and leaned far out over the side to reach, a V-shaped column of tanned muscle, rising wet and steaming from the water.

Claire felt a distinct rush of warmth that was not from the hot water. *Well*, she decided, *why spoil the mood?* Let Jake keep his secret for now.

How long Zoey had lain in her bed just staring blankly at her hand curled up in front of her face, she had no idea. She'd tried to think, to reason it all through, but her thoughts had come in disjointed bits and pieces that ran through her brain over and over and over again.

Pointless, circular thoughts that wouldn't go away. Memories of a friend at school in seventh grade, confessing that her parents were breaking up; the framed wedding picture from her dad's dresser with him in pathetic sideburns and her mother in a white veil; visions of her friends when they found out—Nina, Lucas . . . Jake; her own breakup from Jake; her possible breakup with Lucas; heartbreaking visions of her father when he learned the truth; and Benjamin. What about her brother?

At some point she must have just shut down. She remembered that she had felt a weariness deeper than any she'd ever felt before. But still she was surprised that she had fallen asleep. And surprised that it was now completely dark outside her windows. Downstairs the telephone was ringing.

She stood up, feeling dopey and strange, twisted by a subversive suspicion that she had gone to sleep in one world and awakened in another.

The phone rang again and she stumbled out into the hallway, padding on bare feet over cool wood and carpeting. The house was deserted, silent but for the ringing. On the fourth ring the answering machine came on. From downstairs she could hear the answering message in her father's voice:

Hi, we're not home right now, but since this is an answering machine, you can leave a message after the beep.

The beep came as she was halfway down the stairs. This voice, too, was instantly recognizable:

Um, this is Lucas. I'm just trying to reach Zoey. I would really like to talk to her. So, um, Zoey, if you get this message, I mean, I really wish you would call because . . . I just, like, wish you would call, okay? I . . . um, I love you. Okay? So call me. Bye.

He had mumbled the word *love*, no doubt anticipating that her mother or father might be the first to hear the message. She'd nearly run to catch him before he hung up, but something had held her back. She didn't know what to say to him, not now. Not when the entire universe had been altered and she was still trying to figure out what things meant. How could she know what to say to Lucas? How could she know how she felt about him?

She went into the kitchen and saw the little red message light flashing on the answering machine. Lucas's voice, bottled up there, ready to be replayed. Waiting for her to decide whether she would release it.

So much was waiting for her decision. Lucas waited for her call. Her mother must be waiting, too, for her decision. A family—no, *two* families—waited for her to tell the truth of what she had seen and destroy them. The world she had known, twisted beyond recognition and without warning by her own mother, now waited on her, Zoey Passmore, to complete the destruction.

She was entirely alone: no Lucas, no Nina, no Benjamin. No answers. No reasons. No explanations. Probably there was no explanation. How *could* there be a rational explanation for her mother doing this?

But if there were some reason, she decided, she would do whatever it took to uncover it.

Two

Lucas was sitting on the bed in the condo, staring at the phone, when Nina Geiger went in tentatively, feeling awkward and out of place in the guys' room.

The sun had long since sunk behind the mountains, plunging the pristine little village into twinkling night. Downstairs the others—Aisha and Christopher, Claire and Jake, and Benjamin—were getting ready to go out to eat. Nina and Benjamin had considered staying in, a sort of protest over Zoey's absence, but in the end that had seemed silly. Zoey was a big girl. By now she was back home on the island, probably pouting and crying a little and raging at Lucas for being an insensitive lout.

The insensitive lout was looking haunted and depressed. "Still no one there. I got the answering machine," Lucas said without being asked. "I tried her this morning, no answer. I tried her at lunch, no answer."

"Did you leave a message?" Nina asked.

"Yeah," Lucas said snidely. "I said 'Sorry I tried to pressure you into sleeping with me; can we still be friends?' I'm sure she wouldn't mind her mom or dad getting that message by accident."

"That was sarcasm, right?" Nina asked. She spotted a plaid shirt hanging in the closet. "Is this yours? Can I borrow it for tonight?"

Lucas hung his head. "Sorry. I shouldn't take it out on you. Actually, this last time I *did* leave a message. I told her . . . you know."

"The *L* word?"

"Yeah. I'll sound totally pathetic if her mom hears it. Or her dad, oh man."

Nina busied herself with trying on the shirt in front of the mirrored closet door. Not bad. Looked kind of tough with the rest of her outfit and the eternally unlit Lucky Strike hanging from the corner of her mouth. "She'll get the message before her folks," Nina said reassuringly. *Maybe*, she added silently.

She was at a loss as to why she had come up here after Lucas. Her thinking had been that she would have talked to Zoey if Lucas had gotten through, but now that seemed like a fairly idiotic idea. What would she have been able to say to Zoey? Nina wasn't the reigning world's expert on relationships. What she really wanted was to get the complete story, the detailed word-by-word version that Zoey, as her best friend, was obligated to give her. But that would probably have to wait until Nina got home to the island.

"I guess Benjamin's pissed at me, huh?" Lucas asked.

The question surprised Nina. Lucas had asked it because she was Benjamin's girlfriend and therefore, presumably, an expert on his feelings. It gave Nina a little rush of pleasure that she was accepted in that role. "He just thinks the whole thing is kind of ludicrous. He doesn't think you're scum or anything. He just thinks you're . . ." The phrase Benjamin had actually used was "all hormones and no brain." But that would sound a little harsh. "He just thinks you're kind of impatient."

"Yeah, well, he's not wrong. I *was* impatient. And it is totally ludicrous. You know, she didn't have to run off, though. It's not like I was trying to force her or anything. I mean, I'm not some dog. But now everyone's giving me these looks like I'm Conan the Barbarian trying to jump Snow White."

"Conan the Barbarian tried to jump Snow White?" Nina shook her head. "Not in the Disney version I saw. So I can wear this? I won't get food on it or anything."

"Now what am I supposed to do?" Lucas held up his hands. "She won't even pick up the phone."

"Don't these little problems about . . . you know . . . come up all the time?" Nina asked. "Isn't this all just kind of a normal thing? Like no biggie?"

Lucas shrugged. "I don't know."

"Oh." Somehow she felt Lucas should know. But maybe he wasn't really all that experienced, either.

"I mean, sure, to me sex and all that should just be part of life, right?" he said.

Nina tilted her head back and forth noncommittally. Coming up here had been a mistake.

"I'm a guy, guys like sex. It's normal."

"I've heard that," Nina said.

Lucas spread his hands. "And girls like sex, too, right?"

"Did I just hear Claire calling me?"

His mouth was set in a bitter expression. "Zoey supposedly loves me."

"She does," Nina said confidently. "She's told me so."

A big mistake. Now he was peering at her eagerly. "What else did she tell you?"

"What else?"

"You're her best friend, and you girls tell each other everything. So she must have talked to you about us. What's the deal? Is she planning on being a virgin forever?"

"Ah. Oh, well, I'll tell you, um, Lucas . . ."

"I could use some input here, because it's like we're broken up but I still really love her. Only she never really tells me what she's thinking. At least not about sex. So I don't know. Is this it? Is it totally over? I can't deal with that. I mean, I really can't deal with that."

Nina saw what looked like tears welling up in his eyes, but Lucas turned away and raised his sleeve in what could, arguably, have just been wiping his nose. *That's the way guys are*, Nina told herself, aware that she was learning a great truth—*they'd rather you thought they were wiping snot on their sleeves than admit they were crying*.

A thought occurred to her, and she looked at the sleeve of the shirt she was wearing. It looked clean.

"Maybe you could call," Lucas said, suddenly animated by a new hope. "If she's there, she'll talk to you."

"I don't think I should get involved in this, Lucas."

"Come on, it won't be any big deal. Just call her, and then if she answers, you put me on."

Nina shook her head decisively. "Wrong. Unless I can borrow this shirt. In which case I'll try her later for you."

"It's Christopher's shirt, not mine. Go ahead and take it."

* * *

The lodge restaurant informed them that for a party of seven the wait would be forty-five minutes. If they wanted two separate tables of three and four, they could be seated immediately. That decision was easy—they were hungry. But the decision of how to break down into three and four was more complicated.

Nina and Benjamin wanted to be together. So did Claire and Jake. But Nina and Claire preferred not to be in the same group. Christopher wanted to sit with Aisha, but Aisha made a point of saying she didn't care whom she sat with. And basically, although no one wanted to say it out loud and hurt his feelings, no one wanted to sit with Lucas, who was walking around like a storm cloud on two legs.

Finally they broke up into a group consisting of Nina, Benjamin, and Aisha, and a second group of Claire, Jake, Christopher, and Lucas.

"Well," Nina said, settling into a seat near the huge fireplace that dominated the rustically decorated room, "Claire looks like the slut of the month. Her and three guys at one table."

"What does that make Benjamin here?" Aisha pointed out. "He has two girls." She opened her menu. "Man, do you believe these prices?"

"They're outrageous," Benjamin agreed. He had his menu upside down. "And I don't see anything I want, either."

"Do that to the waitress when she gets here," Nina suggested.

"Uh-uh, not me," Benjamin said. "I was raised in a restaurant family. My folks would kick me out of the house if they found out I hassled a waitress. Or tipped less than fifteen percent."

Nina leaned close to Aisha. "Is Christopher giving you death looks, or is it just my imagination?"

Aisha refused to look toward the other table. She shrugged. "I don't really care."

"Okay," Nina said. "So did you two have a good time skiing today?"

"She says, subtly prying," Benjamin remarked in an undertone.

"Was I being subtle?" Nina asked. "Sorry. What I should have said is, Eesh, what's the deal with you and Christopher? One minute you're on, then you're off, then you're on? You're confusing everyone."

"I wasn't with Christopher today."

"She says, answering an earlier question." Benjamin again.

"I had a private lesson with my friend Peter. Peter from Estonia," Aisha said. "He's trying for a spot on the U.S. Olympic ski team. I met him at the club last night. I'm going to have the fish." She closed her menu decisively.

"She's making Christopher jealous," Benjamin explained to Nina. "Do they have lasagna, by any chance? I feel like lasagna."

"Yeah. It comes with salad."

"Maybe I'm making Christopher jealous," Aisha said, "and maybe I just happen to think Peter from Estonia is cute."

"Where is Estonia, anyway?" Nina asked.

"Or maybe I've just realized that Christopher isn't the only available guy in the world."

"It's a little country right between Latvia and Russia," Benjamin said. "Or else Lithuania."

"Like there's a difference," Nina said to Benjamin. "No, you're right, Aisha—there are lots of available guys around. Like Lucas, if he doesn't perform some very convincing groveling for Zoey."

Aisha waved a hand dismissively. "Oh, they'll

work that out. Lucas's hormones just got a little out of control. A little testosterone poisoning."

Benjamin grinned. "Isn't that the same thing Christopher has? Must be going around. Like the flu."

Nina reached across and felt Benjamin's forehead. "Nope. No symptoms here yet."

"Funny, Nina," Benjamin said. "Funny, and I believe slightly insulting."

"Only slightly?"

Nina felt Benjamin's leg touch hers under the table. She confirmed the pressure and casually wrapped her ankles around his.

"The thing is," Aisha said, "it's necessary in any relationship for there to be certain ground rules. Some basic understandings. Like a constitution that lays out the rights and responsibilities of both people."

"And by making Christopher jealous you're basically writing a constitution?" Benjamin asked, incredulous.

"Exactly," Aisha said. "Just call me Thomasina Jefferson."

"Jefferson was Declaration of Independence," Benjamin said. "Not Constitution."

"Or was it Latvia?" Nina said.

Aisha was undeterred. "We the two people in this relationship, in order to establish a more perfect union, insure domestic tranquility, provide for each of us to always have a date for Saturday night, promote a common defense against being asked out by geeks, and secure the blessings of blistering hot make-out sessions—"

Nina fanned herself with her menu. "I can't wait till we get to the Bill of Rights." She wondered if Benjamin would want to make out tonight. Was he tired of it after last night? She wasn't. She'd never thought she'd feel that way, but she definitely wasn't tired of kissing Benjamin. In fact, she wanted to reach across the table and touch his hand right now.

"Article One—what goes around, comes around. Whatever you can do, I can do back, and harder."

Nina rolled her eyes. "Benjamin, should we just go ahead and break up now, before I end up like Aisha or Zoey?"

"I'm fine," Aisha said. "Don't blame me just because Christopher's a faithless snake and I have to teach him a lesson. And it's not Zoey's fault that Lucas is trying to . . . to . . ."

"Test his equipment?" Nina suggested.

"I hope she's okay," Benjamin said, suddenly sounding concerned.

"Zoey? Come on, Zoey's indestructible," Aisha said.

Nina glanced at her watch. "By now she's gotten past crying over Lucas. She's already constructing some big scenario in her mind about how romantic it will be when she and Lucas make up."

"Yeah, you're probably right," Benjamin agreed. "After all, it's just a little lovers' quarrel. It's only dramatic because we're all here and in order to get some distance from Lucas she had to go all the way home. I was just thinking she has no one to talk to. But I guess she could talk to Mom."

Aisha made a disbelieving face. "Talk to your mom about her boyfriend trying to—"

"Catch up on his sex-ed homework?" Nina suggested. "Practice for his new job as a Trojan tester?"

Benjamin shrugged. "My mom's basically pretty cool. And Zoey gets along okay with her. As long as she doesn't ask my dad, no one will get hurt."

"You know, if I'd been raised in your family, I'd

probably be a much more normal, conventional, and, frankly, boring person,'' Nina said a little wistfully.

''Yeah, but then you and I couldn't go out,'' Benjamin pointed out.

''I wouldn't want that,'' Nina said. She'd intended to toss off the line almost sarcastically. But it came out wobbly with sincerity.

''Me neither,'' Benjamin said, just as seriously.

''Good.''

''Yeah.''

''Definitely,'' Nina said, feeling a warm flush of contentment.

Aisha rolled her eyes. ''You're going to make me lose my appetite,'' she said disgustedly. ''You two are no fun anymore.''

Three

Zoey had slept some more and then gone out for a walk in the cool evening, wandering the utterly familiar streets of North Harbor, Chatham Island's little village, which felt utterly *un*familiar. Were these really the same streets? Really the same small shops, many boarded up, awaiting the next summer's tourists? The same circle, with its grass stunted by the cold, ornamented by the small marble monument to the island's few war dead? The same grocery store window spilling overbright fluorescence onto the street?

It was as if everything had changed, but only slightly, around the edges, so that the illusion of normalcy remained but was ultimately unconvincing. It felt to Zoey as though every building had been moved off-center, that every wall had a newly discovered slant. The faces of the people inside the grocery store, harshly shadowed, were all faces of people she knew and yet alien, hiding darkness and deception.

Car traffic on the island was so infrequent that an approaching car could be heard blocks away. Zoey heard the McRoyans' truck before it entered the circle. It could only be heading to the grocery store.

Where else was there to drive on a Sunday night?

She meant to retreat into the shadows but for some reason stood her ground. The truck came into view—Fred McRoyan, Jake's father, and Jake's ten-year-old sister, Holly. The truck slowed. Holly caught her eye and smiled. Mr. McRoyan seemed not to have noticed Zoey and drove past.

Jake. Something about him tugged at her memory. There had been some argument with Jake, hadn't there? Up in Vermont, what seemed a lifetime ago now. An argument over something. Something of no importance now. So many things that *had* seemed important had now shrunk to insignificance.

Her house was still empty and dark when she returned, but Zoey drew her hand back from the light switch. There was something comforting about the darkness. She moved around familiar objects and through familiar doorways to the kitchen. The answering machine now showed three messages. She almost decided not to play them, but she didn't want them waiting on the machine for her parents to hear. She pressed the *play* button and again heard the same earlier message from Lucas. It was followed by a second message from him. "*It's me again. Look, I'll be home tomorrow, but I'd like to talk to you tonight. Are you there? If you are, pick up, okay? All right, I was a jerk. Is that what you're waiting for? I'm sorry. Just call me, okay?*"

Behind that message came Nina's voice. "*Hey, Zo. If you're there, pick up. Come on, I know you're there. Where else would you be? Look, why don't you call Lucas? Everyone's treating him like dirt and saying he ruined the trip by being a horny little toad; sorry, Mr. and Ms. P., if you're listening. At dinner we made him sit in a corner and eat nothing but crackers. Anyway, he's major-league bummed, and he said if I called you and got you to call him he'd arrange to have Claire killed for me. So come on, Zoey. Please? Call the boy.*"

Zoey listened impassively to the messages. It was odd, really, how much things had changed. Yesterday evening the big question of her life had been whether or not she would sleep with Lucas. Now . . . She laughed mirthlessly. It wasn't *her* sex life—or lack of one—that had turned out to be important. Whatever she might have done with Lucas, it wouldn't have changed the reality of what was going on behind her . . . and her *father's* . . . back.

She should tell him. Her father had a right to know. Didn't he? At least that way he could *do* something.

Yes, he could do something. He could divorce her mother. And possibly destroy a second family as well.

No matter how often she tried to attack the question and come to some kind of a conclusion, it always slipped away into a dense tangle of conflicting loyalties and speculation. And each attempt left her feeling dirty and even sick. It was gross beyond belief to even have to think about any of this.

Zoey went upstairs to her bedroom. She turned on the light and went to the deeply dormered window where she had a built-in desk. Her *father* had built the desk for her, and she had always loved the private, cozy little alcove. The window looked down the length of Camden Street through the silent, moonlit heart of North Harbor.

Her eyes were drawn to the yellow Post-it notes she used to tack quotations onto one side wall of the dormer.

> The world is a comedy to those who think; a tragedy to those who feel.

Yes, she should try to stick to thinking. Stay away from feeling. Zoey pulled down the note and the others beside it, crumpled them in a ball, and dropped them in her trash basket.

She sat down at the desk and opened the drawer. Inside was the journal she used to write her romance novel, or at least the first chapter. She'd written the first chapter over and over again, maybe twenty times. Glancing back through it was like looking back at a slightly distorted record of her own love life. Through most of it, the heroes had a lot in common with Jake. Then there had been a period where she had tried out different models. And the last attempt had featured someone much like Lucas.

All of it naive and ridiculous. Romance novels were just escapism for people who didn't want to face life the way it really was, where "romance" was a boyfriend angrily demanding sex, and where even marriage ended in squalid betrayal.

The journal made a loud noise as it dropped into the trash. Then she got up and searched through her bookshelf, finding the small pink volume half-obscured between larger books. *A Mother's Diary*.

She opened to the first page. A photograph of her mother, very young, holding an extraordinarily tiny baby. Below the photograph, her name—Zoey Elena

Passmore. And written on faint pink lines, the time and date of her birth, her weight, her length from head to doll-size feet.

The pages were decorated with baby blocks and teddy bears and covered with handwriting. It was a notebook her mother had started on the day Zoey was born. She'd written Zoey a letter then, and since that time had added other letters, one on each birthday. On her sixteenth birthday her mother had given it privately to Zoey. Her mother had been a little sheepish, a little embarrassed. But when Zoey had read it, she'd cried.

It had been a testament to her mother's love and to the enduring strength of their family.

Zoey turned to the second page. She read the first paragraph.

Dear Zoey:

Hi, it's me, your mom. Your ***mom.*** *It seems very strange to write that to you because right now you're not even one day old and even though I've held you a couple of times, you don't seem quite real yet. At this point*

Suddenly, a memory. She leafed ahead swiftly in the book. Something . . .

Yes. There it was, on the page devoted to her eighth birthday. "I heard about this island from a person I used to know a long time ago. He seemed to think it's the perfect place to raise kids."

A person I used to know a long time ago. The *same* person? That *same* man?

Zoey placed the notebook gently alongside her journal in the trash. It was part of the past now. Irrelevant.

Unless . . . Unless the past *was* important, at least in this case. "A person I used to know a long time ago." Was that where the explanation was to be found? Had Zoey just discovered something that had been going on for years? If so, then the situation was even worse than she'd imagined.

Her parents were both at the restaurant. There was no chance that either would be home in the next hour. Benjamin was hundreds of miles away in Vermont. She was alone in the house.

What she was now planning to do was wrong, but then, her mother was no longer a person to be talking about right and wrong.

The entrance to the attic was through the ceiling of her parents' walk-in closet. A rope pull with a wooden handle hung down. She tugged at it and down came the plywood stairs with a creak and a cascade of dust and mildew smells. Up, carefully, heart pounding. Fumbling in the dark for the light switch. Sudden illumination from a bare bulb whose harsh light didn't reach the farthest corners. Cardboard boxes, discarded furniture, her old dollhouse coated with dust. She sneezed violently. And again.

She knew just the box. She had found her mother up here once, years ago, sitting cross-legged on the wood floor, reading letters. Supposedly her mother had been getting down the Christmas decorations. It was her mother's job because her father had allergies. He couldn't stand the dust.

Her mother had quickly put away the letters and accepted Zoey's help bringing down the tree stand and the box of lights and gold-foil ropes.

Now Zoey found the box, knelt down, and opened it. A pile of old high school yearbooks. Notebooks. A black mortarboard from her mother's college graduation. Letters, held together with rubber bands.

Zoey lifted the letters. Letters from her grandmother to her mother. Letters from Jeff Passmore to Darla Williams, her mother's maiden name.

And in the middle of the pile, three letters.

From Fred McRoyan to Darla Williams.

To my daughter:

It's your eighth birthday, Zoey. We had a party here at our new house. We had cake and frozen yogurt, which melted. Couldn't get you all the presents you wanted because money is kind of tight right now. Your dad and I bought you clothes, mostly.

We just moved to this island a little while ago. Your dad and I think it will be a good place to raise you and Benjamin, and we're going to open a little restaurant, which is where all your birthday money went. Sorry, honey. We'll try and make it up to you later.

You're a very beautiful little girl, of course. Very mature for eight. You say you're going to be a veterinarian when you grow up. Either that or a philosopher. Where you got that idea I can't imagine. Your father, no doubt.

It looks like you're starting to make friends here. There's a little girl named Claire who seems sweet. Although she has a little sister who just drew mustaches on your old Barbie dolls. You got very upset. I guess by the time you're reading this you'll have gotten over it. But if it turns out the sixteen-year-old you can't stand this Nina girl, at least you'll know how it started.

It's always strange when I write in this book. I mean, here you are right now, a little girl, and I'm writing to you when you'll be a young woman. I don't have any idea what your life will be like then, although I hope it's wonderful and that you're happy.

If we manage to stay here on the island, I believe it will

work out. This is like a safe place in the world. A long way from all the things that could hurt you or Benjamin.

If not, I guess I'm to blame. I heard about this island from a person I used to know a long time ago. He seemed to think it's the perfect place to raise kids.

Anyway, so far I have a perfect little girl.

Four

Zoey's mother was at the breakfast table the next morning, reading the paper as always, drinking coffee. Zoey's father was already down at the restaurant. It was the Monday of a three-day weekend.

Her mother said hello in her usual way. Zoey said hello back and fixed herself a bowl of Grape-Nuts. She sat down at the table, tugging at the back of the Boston Bruins jersey she wore to bed. She had halfway decided she wouldn't sit with her mother, but that would be cowardly. She wasn't going to start acting like she was afraid to be around her. It was her mother who should feel guilty. It was her mother who owed her an explanation.

But her mother just turned the page with a rustling of newsprint and sipped again at her coffee.

Zoey ate her cereal. Her mother drank coffee. The silence was like a vise that kept tightening, squeezing, increasing the pressure in the room.

Zoey choked on a mouthful of cereal and had to clear her throat repeatedly.

"You shouldn't eat so fast," her mother said from behind the paper.

"Don't tell me what to do," Zoey snapped. Resentment boiled up inside her. She glared at the blank gray wall of newspaper. There was a computer sale at Circuit City.

"Suit yourself," her mother said with supreme indifference.

"I will." God, how she wanted a fight. How she wanted to get it out in the open and tell her mother just what she thought of her. To hurl accusation after accusation, each phrase carefully crafted and rehearsed and replayed during the night when she should have been sleeping. Just let her mother say *anything* even remotely critical. Anything that would serve as an excuse for Zoey to unload the razor-sharp verbal spears.

Her mother sipped her coffee. Zoey ate her cereal, barely chewing, not tasting at all.

The phone rang and Zoey jerked. Her mother's paper responded as well.

A second ring.

"It's probably for you," her mother said.

"Maybe it's Daddy," Zoey said.

A third ring.

Her mother sighed. "I don't think your father would be calling me."

"Maybe he wants to find out what you're up to," Zoey said with a cold sneer.

A fourth ring.

The answering machine came on. Her father's voice on the outgoing message. A beep. A click.

"Hi, it's me, Lucas. Um, Zoey, in case you were going to call me here, don't, okay? Because we're coming home. We're leaving right now because it's started to rain. So I'll be home soon and we can, you know, maybe we could talk and work everything out, okay? I mean, look, I understand your feelings and I

respect them, so don't get all down. Everything will be cool. We can—''

A beep. The message had run over thirty seconds.

The sound of the tape rewinding.

Zoey was finished with her cereal. Her mother's cup was empty.

Her mother put down her paper, slowly, deliberately. She met Zoey's eye and didn't flinch. ''Is there something you want to talk about, Zoey?''

Zoey stared at her. ''What could I possibly want to talk about?''

''I don't know. You seemed—''

''You know,'' Zoey said quietly. Then, in a voice near a shriek, ''You *know* what there is to talk about!''

At last her mother looked away. A bitter smile tugged at the corners of her mouth but failed. ''You don't understand everything, Zoey. You're still just a kid.''

''You're right. I don't understand. I wish I did, but I don't.''

Her mother was quiet for a while. She sat with shoulders slumped and head low, staring blindly toward a corner of the linoleum. ''Look, I love your father.''

Zoey let out a short bark of a laugh. Of course she did. That's why twenty years ago she'd been getting letters from Mr. McRoyan and yesterday she'd been . . .

She hadn't read the letters. Not yet, and she wasn't sure she would or even could. But she didn't have to read them to guess that they were love letters.

''Well, believe what you want to believe,'' her mother said. ''You will anyway.''

"What if I tell Daddy?" The threat was out of her mouth before she realized it.

It didn't have the devastating effect she had expected. Her mother raised her eyebrows, then just looked thoughtful. "I don't know. Is that what you're going to do?"

Zoey searched for some fierce response, but none came to mind. She felt deflated. She'd never talked this way to her mother before, and far from being a liberating experience, it left her feeling hollow. "I don't know what I'm going to do."

Her mother stood up, lifting herself heavily from the table. She carried her coffee cup to the dishwasher. With her back to Zoey she said, "Don't be too quick to judge. Later in life you may find that living up to your high ideals isn't easy. That life is more about shades of gray than it is about black and white. And then you'll regret that you weren't more generous on the day you discovered your mother was just human."

Five

Lucas did most of the driving on the way back from Vermont. It was the best way to avoid being next to Jake and Claire, and Nina and Benjamin, who were holding hands and occasionally kissing and in general reminding him of the fact that he alone had managed to actually scare his girlfriend clear into another state.

Thank God for Christopher and Aisha, proof that at least part of the human race could act with some restraint. Although, given their unpredictable relationship, it wouldn't be surprising to see them all over each other suddenly. Aisha loved to talk about being logical and sensible, but there had never been more than about ten logical minutes between those two since they'd met.

Lucas hadn't slept much. He'd spent the waking hours of night swinging back and forth between self-righteous anger and self-pitying remorse. Now he was just feeling washed out, tired, sick of his friends, sick of himself, sick of everything.

He pulled off the highway, decelerating into the off-ramp, glad to be almost home.

Weymouth was surrounded by a ring of suburban sprawl, a jumbled wasteland of golden arches and red-roofed Pizza Huts, gas station price marquees, shabby banners over used-car dealerships, power lines, orange U-Haul trucks, discount stores, and mud-spattered cars. Within this ring was a second layer of older two-story homes, painted off-white and off-yellow and a shade that might have been a type of green or gray or just a deliberate attempt at ugliness. Bare trees and sparse, dying grass defined yards littered with Big Wheels and unused garden hoses.

Maine at this time of year, after the trees had lost their brilliant leaves and before the first cleansing snows, was not a pretty sight, Lucas decided glumly. Although, if Zoey had been beside him . . .

He veered to avoid a lunatic in a Volvo. Massachusetts plates, he noted. Inevitably.

They came to the edge of the city center, a small cluster of ten- and fifteen-story buildings that overlooked the Portside area. Here everything had been given over to yuppies and tourists—red brick, smoked glass, cobblestones, slick, understated corporate logos and professionally quaint hand-lettered signs.

"Damn it!"

Lucas glanced up in his rearview mirror. The outburst had come from Christopher. He was turned around in his seat, staring hard at traffic moving in the opposite direction.

"Give me some paper and a pen, anything!" he demanded of Aisha.

"What is it?"

"Quick. Before I forget." While Aisha dug in her purse, Christopher began reciting a string of letters and numbers over and over again.

A license number, Lucas realized.

Aisha produced a scrap of paper and a pencil. Christopher scribbled furiously. "Got 'em. Got 'em.

GOT the sons of bitches! Brice Street. That's where they turned.''

''What have you got?'' Nina asked curiously.

Christopher's eyes were cold. ''It was them,'' he said. ''I'm sure. I saw the guy driving, the skinhead, racist piece of crap. And now I have his license number.'' He waved the scrap of paper like it was a winning lottery ticket.

Lucas felt a sinking sensation. ''Christopher, I thought you never got a good look at the guys.''

''It was him,'' Christopher said staunchly. ''It was that guy back there in that raggedy old Ford. One of them, anyway.''

Christopher had been very badly beaten up in an attack by a gang of skinheads who had seen him talking to Zoey. Zoey had been unable to identify the assailants. But Lucas knew who was behind the assault—a damaged little creep he had known while he was in the Youth Authority juvenile jail. A little psychopath who had earned the nickname Snake for very good reasons.

''Now you can go to the cops,'' Jake said, becoming alert after a nap in the back. He too had caught the dangerous tone in Christopher's voice. ''Give them the number. Let them handle it.''

''Yeah, they were so good at handling it the first time,'' Christopher said sarcastically.

''You have a lead now,'' Lucas said. ''They'll check it out.''

Christopher nodded. ''Uh-huh. You're right. That's what I'll do. I'll go to the cops.''

''Don't do anything stupid,'' Aisha said in a low voice.

''Not me,'' Christopher said. He carefully folded the scrap of paper and put it in his pocket.

* * *

Benjamin took five minutes to say good-bye to Nina after they stepped off the ferry. It was slightly idiotic, since Nina would probably be over at his house within an hour, but basically he didn't care. He liked kissing Nina good-bye, hello, or whatever.

For Benjamin it was a relief to be back on the island. The island was familiar turf, a gridwork of streets measured out in steps and stored in his memory. It was a place he could move around confidently, without reliance on guides or even much on his cane. The path from the ferry landing to his home was one he knew well—so many steps to cross the square, so many steps up the slow incline of Exchange Street, a sharp right, watch out for the uneven brick sidewalk, so many more steps along Camden to the gate, to the door, to his room on the ground floor.

He slung his bag onto his bed, pulled off his jacket, hanging it on the seventh hanger from the left, and found the remote control for his stereo precisely where he had left it on the corner of his rolltop desk. He ran his fingers along the rack of CDs, found the section devoted to classical music, found the Braille tag on the spine of one CD, and inserted it in the changer.

Bach whispered in a corner. He adjusted the volume with his remote and Bach filled the room with elegant, deeply satisfying precision.

Finally. After an entire weekend of Nina's music—Nine Inch Nails, Pearl Jam, Blues Traveler, Chili Peppers . . . Fine music, but not Bach. He liked Nina. He liked her a lot. Maybe he was getting beyond liking. But he was going to have to do something about her taste in music.

Of course, she thought the same about him.

For a moment he tried to picture Nina. He had the bare facts. He knew that her hair was dark brown, that her eyes were gray. He knew that she was only of average height.

People said she was very pretty and then almost always seemed to add a "but." Pretty, but doesn't act like it. Pretty, but seems to want to hide the fact. And the inevitable pretty, but of course, not like Claire.

But to Benjamin, who had at one time dated Claire and was now with Nina, the question of whether or not Nina was quite as beautiful as Claire was less important than the fact that when he kissed Nina, her heart pounded wildly, extravagantly. That her breath was burning hot against his cheek. That she sometimes made this little, involuntary, unconscious whimpering sound when he kissed the curve where her neck and cheek met.

Nina was hot to Claire's cold. Warm. Sweet. Funny. With very, very soft lips.

The knock on his door startled him, though it was gentle enough.

"Yeah?"

"I guess you're back." Zoey's voice.

"No one can fool you for long," Benjamin said. "Come on in."

The sound of the door opening, a long complaining squeak. Benjamin deliberately never let the door hinges be oiled. The squeaks were useful clues.

"Hi," Zoey said.

"So you did make it back. The way you kept refusing to return Lucas's phone calls, we weren't sure."

"I just didn't feel like calling," Zoey said.

Her voice was low, uncharacteristically grim. "You're not still upset over that, are you?" An unwelcome thought occurred to Benjamin. "Wait a minute. Something else didn't happen between you and Lucas, did it?"

"No. It wasn't like that. We just had a little disagreement."

Oh? Benjamin thought. It's *just* a little disagreement? Then why did she sound like her batteries were about dead?

"So. You're fine?" he asked.

"Sure. Why wouldn't I be?"

A definite false note. Maybe she just felt embarrassed over the way she had run off. It *had* been a little extreme. "You'll be happy to know that Lucas has been crawling around like he's lost the meaning of his life."

"Yeah, well . . . whatever. Are you hungry?"

Benjamin's jaw dropped open, but he recovered quickly. Okay. She didn't want to talk about Lucas. Fine. But she sounded nearly indifferent. Which made no sense at all. This was Zoey, after all. Zoey, who disappeared with Lucas into her room every afternoon and emerged for dinner humming and singing and twirling around and suddenly blurting out profound questions like, "Do you think love just keeps growing, or does it reach some ultimate point and that's as far as it can grow?" Or "Is love just a really strong form of like, or is it completely separate?"

Now it was ". . . whatever"? Something was definitely going on with his little sister.

"Yeah, I am hungry," Benjamin said. "I thought maybe we'd head down to the restaurant. Reassure Mom and Dad that I made it home alive and didn't even get a tattoo or anything."

"There's food here," Zoey said, too quickly. "I'll make you something."

Ah. Trouble with their parents? Zoey? Almost as unlikely as her indifference toward Lucas.

He shrugged. Whatever it was, it would come out sooner or later. Or more likely, given Zoey's naturally sunny disposition, her mood would just evaporate. And in the meantime, he *was* hungry.

"Okay. Let's raid the refrigerator."

Six

"So, Claire, did you and Benjamin have a good time in Vermont?" Mr. Geiger asked, forking up a piece of salmon. "I don't suppose Benjamin could ski at all. Could he?"

Claire paused with her own fork hovering over her plate. She noticed the way Nina, sitting across the table, winced and gagged on a mouthful of soda. Janelle, the Geiger family's housekeeper and cook, cocked an ear as she set up dessert and coffee on the sideboard.

"I'm not seeing Benjamin anymore," Claire said.

"Oh." Her father looked confused. "Did I know that already?"

"It may have been mentioned," Claire said. Then, with a beatific smile at Nina, who was urgently shaking her head *no*, Claire added, "Benjamin's seeing someone else now."

Mr. Geiger shrugged. "His loss," he said loyally.

"But you might still get him as a son-in-law someday," Claire added.

"Really? Oh, I see. You think you'll get back together with him? That would be fine, I like that boy. Sharp as a bayonet."

Nina's eyes were narrowed, glaring daggers, so naturally Claire had to go on. "Yes, we all like Benjamin. Don't we, Nina?"

Nina stabbed her knife into her fish and twisted the blade.

"*Especially* Nina."

Mr. Geiger looked even more confused. "Why especially Nina?"

Claire shrugged. "She's the one who's going out with him."

Nina's appalled embarrassment was as rewarding as Claire had hoped. Nina loved to go around provoking other people, but of course couldn't stand to have details of her private life brought up in front of their father.

Mr. Geiger's eyebrows shot up. He looked at Nina. Looked at Claire. Looked back at Nina.

"She stole him away from me," Claire said sadly, fighting to suppress a grin.

Nina was turning red, nearly choking on her food.

"Broke my heart," Claire added for good measure.

"What heart?" Nina growled.

Mr. Geiger looked embarrassed. "This is . . . Not that I want to tell you girls how to run your romantic lives, but, well, it's a bit tacky."

"It's your own fault, Claire," Nina said. "Benjamin told you repeatedly that he was not ready to have kids."

Mr. Geiger stabbed his tongue with his fork.

Okay, Claire admitted to herself, *that was good.* You had to hand it to Nina—the little psycho was quick.

Nina held up her right hand and, using her palm to hide what she was doing from their father, gave Claire the finger with her other hand.

Mr. Geiger, apparently sensing that he had once

again stumbled into the middle of the ongoing cold war between his daughters, sighed, gave Janelle a look, and concentrated on eating his dessert.

After dinner Nina pursued Claire up the stairs. "Hey, you're not really upset that I'm going with Benjamin, are you?"

"Not in the least," Claire said. Only a very partial lie. Mostly true. It would have been nice if somehow her previous boyfriends could live out their lives pining miserably, but that wasn't realistic. Lucas was with Zoey, Benjamin with Nina. When it grew tired between Jake and her, he'd probably find another girlfriend, too.

"Damn. I knew it was too much to hope for," Nina said.

Claire paused. "I *was* a little upset at first, because I couldn't imagine how, after being with me, he could find you at all interesting or satisfying. Then I realized it was just part of a bigger trend."

She left Nina behind on the second-floor landing and climbed toward her own third-floor room.

"Okay, like a moron, I'll bite," Nina said, pursuing her. "What trend?"

Claire shrugged. "Oh, people give up real butter for margarine, real ice cream for frozen yogurt, real steak for tofu burgers. I mean, they tell themselves it's almost as good as the real thing, but of course, we all know they're just trying to make themselves feel good."

"So, you're Häagen-Dazs—"

"And you're store-brand nonfat vanilla frozen yogurt."

"You're fat, then, and I'm nonfat," Nina said thoughtfully. "Okay, if you say so, but I never really thought of you as fat, Claire. Oh, maybe a little in your butt and those oversized buffers of yours. And, of course, your head.''

Another good comeback. This is what came of Nina spending more time with Benjamin. She was growing more confident, harder to throw off-guard. It was very annoying.

They were at the door to Claire's room. ''Scat,'' she said. ''Shoo.''

''I wanted to ask you something,'' Nina said. ''Seriously.''

Claire made a face. She didn't want to invite Nina in, but Claire had recently promised that if Nina needed someone to talk to, she'd be there for her. It was a promise made in the emotional aftermath of Nina's revelations about their uncle. And now Claire was stuck with it.

''Come in. Just don't touch anything or sit on my bed.''

Nina followed her in and instantly flopped back on Claire's bed. ''How come Dad doesn't get married again?''

''She asks, changing the subject with her usual grace.''

''Seriously. I mean, he's not a bad-looking old guy. He has lots of money. That's his own hair. He owns several suits, although they all look the same.''

''Just guessing, but maybe he doesn't want to get remarried.''

''We should tell him it's okay with us if he does,'' Nina said. ''I mean, next year you're out of here, off to college, thank-God-and-I'm-counting-the-days. The year after that, boom, I'm out of here, too. Then what does he have?''

''Hmm. A minus followed by a plus,'' Claire said. But actually, this wasn't the first time the question had occurred to her. Burke Geiger didn't have a lot of friends, let alone female friends.

"What did he do while we were away in Vermont? All he does is work and play golf."

Claire looked blank. "I don't know," she admitted.

"And when you and I are gone, it will be like that all the time. Who's going to be around to help him with his walker and buy him his old fart diapers and listen to his boring stories about how great it was when he had his own teeth?"

"Nina, Dad is forty-one."

"Yeah, see? He could live another twenty years, even more. And by then we'll both be off on our own. You'll be a bitter, lonely old lady living with cats."

"And I'll be bringing you magazines and chewing gum on visitors' day at the State Hospital for the Hopelessly Pathetic," Claire said.

"I'm just thinking we give the old man the big okay, you know? Say, 'Hey Dad, we think you're ready to start seeing girls. As long as she doesn't move in till we're out of here and she doesn't mess with my room.' "

Claire nodded. "Would you really be okay with that?"

"It's what Mom would have wanted," Nina said, suddenly serious. "She wouldn't want him to be all alone when we leave."

Tears suddenly appeared in Claire's eyes and she turned away, making a point of looking out the window. Damn. Behind her she heard a discreet snuffle. Their mother had been dead for five years. Maybe in another five the mention of her would no longer bring tears to her daughters' eyes. To this day their father couldn't speak of her without his voice wavering and strangling and dying away.

"Okay," Claire said. "But I'll do it. At the right time and place. I don't want you telling him he'll be senile soon." She made a face. "You know, Nina, I don't like this new, dippy-romantic personality of yours. You're changing for the worse, and I honestly didn't think that was possible."

The day had passed in a daze. Zoey had done her homework, preparing to make the first day back at school as painless as possible. She had watched bad daytime TV. She had eaten too much without tasting any of it. She had listened to music, but even with that, the pervasive sense of strangeness persisted. Halfway through a Mariah Carey album she loved, she turned it off and nearly threw it away. It was all mush and sentimentality. No bearing on the real world.

She had avoided dealing with things. But now, as night fell again, as she finished the dishes from her evening meal with an unusually quiet Benjamin, she was feeling rushed. She couldn't just go on avoiding things.

Upstairs in her room, Zoey almost pulled her notebook from the trash where it lay like a reproach. She needed paper. She needed to think things through and get a grip. But she left the notebook and found an old yellow pad instead.

With a pen she wrote two headings at the top of the page:

Tell   Don't Tell

That's what it came down to. She could tell her father what she had seen, or she could keep quiet.

There wasn't really any middle ground. She felt she should reach some firm decision very soon. Letting things hang was too nerve-wracking. And it would become increasingly impossible to keep Benjamin, who seldom missed anything for long, from prying.

Under Tell she wrote

The truth should come out.

Then, under Don't Tell,

Why should it come out?

Why should the truth come out? Should Nina have to tell everyone she met that she had been molested by her uncle? Should Lucas have to tell everyone that he had spent almost two years in a juvenile prison?

But Lucas had been there because the truth had *not* come out. Not until Claire had recalled the truth and admitted it had things started to get cleared up.

Under Don't Tell she wrote

Truth would probably cause divorce.

But again there was a counterargument. Under Tell she added

Sooner or later Daddy will find out.

The very thought filled her with incalculable bitterness and anger. It would be like a knife in her father's heart.

And the man her mother had been with! How could she have chosen Jake's father, Mr. McRoyan, over Zoey's father? Not to mention the fact that the man in question also had a family.

It was incredible. It was monstrous. It was a sin. That's what her religious friends, Aisha, Lucas . . . Jake . . . yes, that's what Jake would call it. A sin. Adultery. What a tired, old-fashioned word. Adultery. Divorce. The two went together, didn't they? And then what? Separate houses? Living with one parent and visiting the other on weekends, like half the kids at school?

Not her. Not *her* family.

Under Don't Tell:

Maybe it was just once and will never happen again.

Yes, maybe. Her mother knew that Zoey knew. Surely she would never do it again. And then life could go on like normal. Her father wouldn't have to know. Maybe her parents could still be in love.

Or maybe the answer could be found in one of the old letters now stuffed beneath Zoey's pillow. For the thousandth time, Zoey thought about the letters. All through the night she had toyed with the idea of reading them. But did she really want to know what was in them?

She had to know, Zoey rationalized. Had to know what she was dealing with. She pulled out the letters and opened the first one with trembling fingers.

Dearest Darla,

I wish I could have written sooner, but they keep us jumping here, ha ha. Yesterday we took our first low-altitude parachute jump. Scared the hell out of me but it was fun, too.

I'll be getting a pass for next weekend so we can see each other, if you still want to. I guess I can tell you all about it then.

I know you probably are feeling a little uncertain because of what happened between us last weekend. I guess neither one of us planned for it to happen although I'm glad it did.

I know it sounds like I'm just saying this for selfish reasons, but I don't think you have to be faithful to a guy who goes running off to hitchhike through Europe without you. How do you know he's being faithful to you? Answer: You don't. If it was me, I'd never leave you alone.

How are exams coming? Soon you'll have a college degree. Will you even talk to a lowly soldier like me? Ha ha. I hope you will.

Anyway, I can't write much more because it's lights out soon and besides as you can tell I'm not a very great writer. I just want to say that I really miss you, and really care for you. I have a picture of you up beside my bunk and all the guys say you're the prettiest pinup in the barracks.

So please write me back and tell me we can be together again very soon.

Love,
Fred

The door to her room opened a crack. An unlit cigarette appeared, followed slowly by Nina's face, making a dramatic appearance.

Zoey quickly crumpled the letter and slid it under her pillow, feeling a flush of guilt and resentment at Nina for showing up out of nowhere like this.

"Hey, Zoey."

"Uh, hi, Nina."

"Missed you, girl," Nina said. She flopped on Zoey's bed, making Zoey bounce.

"Yeah, me too," Zoey said, trying to sound convincing. She just wasn't ready to start dealing with people yet. She felt trapped in a weird space where normal laws of existence had been suspended. Having Nina show up was like having someone totally unexpected wander through a dream.

"So. Talk to Lucas yet?"

Zoey shook her head. "No, not yet."

"Cool. So?"

"So what?"

"So let's have the blow-by-blow, minute-by-minute. Let's go over the transcript of the fateful scene. I'll set it up. There's you, the shy yet plucky virgin. Then there's Lucas, the lowdown horny dog. Take it from there."

"Oh, that."

"Duh. Like I wouldn't want to hear the whole story. I mean, it ends with the shy yet plucky virgin running clear into another state."

For a moment Zoey's mood lightened. It was hard to resist Nina's direct and completely disrespectful attitude. And the quickest way to get rid of Nina was to do what she wanted. If she tried to blow her off, Nina would turn relentless. "Look, I probably overreacted. Okay, we've had this ongoing—"

"Fight? War? Battle to the death?"

"This disagreement over, you know, the Big Question."

"You mean this is about whether or not Madonna's career is totally finished?"

Zoey felt her mouth smile. The first in what seemed

like forever. Thank God for Nina. "That's right. We were fighting over Madonna."

"Okay, so Lucas was trying to go where no man has gone before. He wanted to carry out an in-depth poll." Nina grinned, waiting.

"I assume you have one more?" Zoey said, playing her part.

"Of course. The three-part comic tautology rule must be observed," Nina said.

"Okay, let's hear it."

"He was gripping his bat, hoping to bang a home run and win one for the zipper."

"Are you done?"

"Actually, I have about eight more."

"The rule is three," Zoey said. "*Your* rule. Comic examples should come in threes, going from least to most funny."

"So basically I have it about right?"

"Basically."

"And you said *no*," Nina prompted, showing impatience with Zoey's delaying tactics.

"That's about it."

"And he said ohplease ohplease ohplease."

Again Zoey smiled. "Actually, he said I wasn't ready to grow up."

"Good shot." Nina nodded.

"And then he demanded to know when I thought I might be ready."

"And you told him—?"

"I'd let him know."

Nina laughed and gave Zoey a slightly off-target high five. "Excellent."

"And then he got mad . . ."

"And you were upset, huh?" This, in a gentler tone

of voice. "Tears? Sobs? Vows of revenge? Plans to make him regret it?"

"I guess I was upset," Zoey said, almost wonderingly. At the time it had seemed a terribly difficult problem. Insoluble.

Nothing compared to what had been waiting for her when she got home.

Nina nodded. Then she looked her friend in the eye. "And it's because of this that you threw your romance notebook and your quotes and that book your mom gave you into the trash?" Nina looked significantly at the trash, then back at Zoey.

Zoey froze. The question had taken her completely by surprise. She'd forgotten about the trash. She knew her face was growing red. "That's right, Nina," she said. "I guess I thought maybe Lucas was partly right. Maybe it *is* time for me to grow up."

Seven

''You know, you could stay one more night,'' Aisha said.

Christopher was looking disconsolately around the room, at the huge carved mahogany four-poster bed, the expensive rugs, the lush draperies, and especially at the oversized incredible bathroom with its raised Jacuzzi. They had just come upstairs from her mother's farewell dinner for Christopher. Mrs. Gray was sorry to see him go. Mr. Gray was relieved.

''Nah. I have to exit to reality sometime,'' Christopher said. He was holding a black nylon zippered bag that contained his belongings. ''Back to my one room with the kitchenette in the corner and the bathroom down the hall.''

''You have an excellent view there,'' Aisha said. ''The beach. The lights of Weymouth.''

''Uh-huh. And I share a moldy stall shower with the other three guys on my floor.''

Aisha patted him on the back. It was obviously hard for him to leave this room, which wasn't exactly a surprise. The room was the prize jewel in her mother's bed-and-breakfast. In summer it rented out to tourists for two hundred or so a day. After Christopher's assault, Aisha's parents had allowed him to stay here and recuperate.

The truth was, Aisha herself would have liked to take the room. Her own was considerably less magnificent.

"Oh, well," Christopher said with a shrug. "I'm out of here."

"I'll walk you downstairs."

The night was chilly. A breeze whistled through the bare oak trees and sighed through the needles of the pines. High swift clouds scudded beneath a half-moon.

Christopher piled the bag on his battered bike. "If it keeps getting colder, I'm going to have to buy an island car."

"This is Maine, Christopher. Believe me, it keeps getting colder. Six weeks from now you will not still be delivering papers by bike. Trust me on this."

"Yeah, I guess you're right. Back home in Baltimore you just have a bad month or so."

"You know what they say about Maine. We have two seasons, winter and July. Check the bulletin board at Island Grocery. Someone's always selling an island car. And remember, if it costs more than three hundred bucks or if the seats aren't ripped to shreds, people will think you're showing off."

Christopher grinned. "This is about the only place where I could actually afford to buy a car that would fit in." Island cars were inevitably salt-eaten, rattling, beaten, dented wrecks that ran on half their cylinders, dragged their mufflers, and had license plates from 1970. On Chatham Island, there wasn't much need for driving. People kept their real cars in covered parking garages on the mainland.

"Well, in the meantime be careful. The streets get slippery sometimes."

"Worried about me?" he asked with a winning smile.

"Not really."

"Back to school for you tomorrow. And work for me," Christopher said.

"Uh-huh."

"Interesting weekend. I think if I hadn't still been sore and stiff, I could have really gotten into the whole skiing experience. Plus, if I was rich enough to be able to afford that condo and the meals and the lessons and the ski tickets."

Aisha knew she should just let it drop. He was obviously trying to keep the conversation going. Hoping for what? A kiss? "Yeah, I think it would be fun if I could ski as well as Claire and Zoey. But just taking lessons wasn't any big thrill."

"Really?" He cocked an eyebrow. "Even the lessons you got from Peter the Estonian wonder boy?"

"He did show me a few good tricks," Aisha said, keeping a straight face. Ha. Take that, Christopher I-can't-be-tied-down-to-one-girl Shupe. Mr. That-blond-girl-was-just-someone-I-met.

"Yeah, I'll bet he did." Christopher seemed about to say something else, but instead he just raised his bike and shouldered his bag. "Listen, tell your mom and dad thanks again, okay? Anything I can ever do to repay them—"

"My mom loved it. She has the hospitality gene. Can't stand it when there's no one around to take care of and show off her decorating to."

He nodded. "So." He nodded again, looking down at the ground. "So, I'm going." He pushed his bike across the yard, but at the gate he stopped. Carefully he leaned the bike against the post and came back, walking resolutely toward her.

"I forgot something," he said.

"What?"

"This." He took her in his arms and kissed her. By the time he released her, she was gasping for breath.

Christopher walked away, a new swagger in his step. He stopped at the gate and looked back. "Remember that the next time you're thinking about Peter from Estonia."

"Wait a minute," Aisha said, stopping him in his tracks. She walked across the yard. "I forgot something, too." She reached up with both hands, placing them on his face, and drew him down to her. She kissed him softly, gently, then with more fire and still more. She let a hand drift down slowly over his chest, around his lean waist, over his hard butt, drawing him closer still. Then she released him.

"Now," she said. "*You* remember *that* the next time you want to be a big macho jerk who treats women like they're just numbers to be added up."

Aisha turned sharply and headed back to the house. And if it weren't for the fact that her knees were wobbly and her heart was hammering, she would have felt very pleased with herself.

Lucas was on his deck, looking down toward Zoey's house, when he heard their front door open. From his vantage point he could see only the back of the Passmore house—the unused spare bedroom upstairs, the dining room, kitchen, breakfast nook, and family room downstairs—all of which were dark.

But he could recognize the voice that floated over

the roof of Zoey's house. Nina. Saying good-bye at the front door.

Good. With Nina gone, he could decide whether he was going to get up the nerve to go down and see Zoey. Nina emerged from the lee of the house and was visible briefly, walking with head down along the street. He heard the sound of the door closing.

He should go down right now. Talk all this out before she decided to go to bed early or something. But what was he going to say? That was the problem. Was he going to promise never to try to get her to sleep with him?

Yeah, right. She'd certainly believe that. About like she'd believe that he had decided to become a priest.

No. There wasn't any point in b.s.'ing her. Zoey wasn't stupid. The only thing that would do any good would be to tell her that he would leave it entirely up to her to decide *when* or even *whether*.

But man, that grated on his nerves.

The door opened again, and this time Zoey emerged around the side of the house. She was carrying a white trash bag, which she stuffed into the big plastic garbage bin.

Lucas stepped back silently from the deck rail, melting into shadows. Zoey was staring at the trash as if it had some powerful significance. Her features, in shadow, lit only by refracted moonlight, looked sad. It would have been impossible to interrupt her at this moment, Lucas decided.

Finally, with a dismissive shake of her head, Zoey went back inside. A moment later the kitchen light came on. Zoey went to the refrigerator and, to Lucas's utter amazement, pulled out a beer. She used a towel to help twist off the cap and took a deep swig. Then she made a face. But doggedly she took a second drink. She stared for a while at the bottle, again with a sad, faraway expression.

Lucas heard the whispery sound of a bike coming down Climbing Way, the road that led up the ridge of the hill behind Lucas's home. There was a low squeal of brakes.

In the kitchen below, Zoey took a third drink, barely a sip this time, and drained the rest of the beer into the sink. Lucas smiled. Zoey would never have much of a future as a drunk.

The kitchen light went off.

Behind him Lucas heard a sound. He spun around.

"Ha. Scared you."

Christopher appeared from around the corner of Lucas's house. He was carrying a black nylon bag. He leaned his bike against the deck railing.

"Spying on Zoey?" Christopher asked. "Does she dance around naked down there or something?"

Lucas rolled his eyes tolerantly. "No, but Benjamin does."

"Don't make me sick."

Lucas glanced at the big bag. "Moving out of the Royal Palace?"

Christopher made a face. "Had to happen sooner or later."

"Not necessarily," Lucas said. "If you could keep from pissing off Aisha—"

"Look who's talking. Have you seen Zoey yet?"

Lucas shrugged.

"That's what I figured."

"It's kind of hard . . ."

Christopher immediately broke out laughing.

"It's kind of *difficult*, you sleaze."

"Uh-huh." Christopher shifted uncomfortably. "So, look, Lucas—"

That tone of voice was too familiar to miss. "You'd better not be about to ask me how you can get a gun again," Lucas warned. "We've been over that."

Christopher shook his head. "No, I respect what you said on that. I was just wondering if you know how to trace a license number."

Lucas turned and looked at Christopher. "Give it to the cops; they'll know how it's done."

"Isn't there any other way?"

"Give it to the cops, dude."

"Screw the cops, man," Christopher said heatedly. "This isn't about cops. All right?"

"Chill. My old man's asleep up there." Lucas jerked his head over his shoulder. "I don't want to have to deal with him on top of you."

"Sorry. But see, this isn't something I can just shake off." He stuck a finger in Lucas's face. "Those pricks put me in the hospital."

"Go to the damned cops," Lucas said tersely.

"So they can do what? Bust the guys *maybe*, and *maybe* they stay locked up for twenty-four hours before they make bail and come out looking for me? I'm not that hard to find. It's not like there are a lot of black guys in the area."

Lucas started to argue, but there weren't any arguments he could make. What Christopher didn't realize was that Lucas knew exactly who had beaten him up. Knew their names and records and associates. And he had concealed that information precisely because he was afraid that if he rolled over on the guys, they'd get out on bail and come after the people he cared about. Zoey, to be specific.

Lucas sighed. "I can't tell you that's not how it works out. That is how it works."

"So I either just shut up and take my beating, or what? I move out of the state? I'm not getting pushed around by some skinhead punks."

Lucas was silent. What the hell was he supposed to do? Christopher was his friend. The skins were psychos who'd sooner or later end up shot, serving life, or overdosing on any number of deadly substances. But in the meantime they were dangerous. There was no way he could get into the middle of this. He didn't approve of violence. It sounded naive, but he didn't. He didn't even watch violent movies. Still, if it was down to choosing sides . . .

"You know, Christopher, how sometime some guy might run into your car, then drive off?"

"What?"

"I'm saying suppose your car gets hit by someone who just drives off but you happen to see his license plate number."

Christopher nodded slowly.

"There must be some way to trace a license plate in a case like that. Probably the Department of Motor Vehicles. I mean, if someone did that to my car, I guess I'd call the DMV."

Christopher smiled grimly. "You're a friend, man." He gave Lucas a friendly punch on the shoulder. Soon he was on his bike, heading off into the night.

Lucas looked back down at Zoey's house. The kitchen light was still off. His eyes were drawn to the white plastic bag that Zoey had thrown away, acting as if it was the most important trash in the world.

"I wonder," he murmured, "what that was all about?"

To my daughter,

On your tenth birthday.

I barely know what to write this time, Zoey. This has not been a good year for any of us. Next week we are taking Benjamin down to Boston to have the operation. The surgeon is supposed to be the very best in the country, but he says the tumor is almost impossible to reach. He says Benjamin may die. Or if he does survive, he may be permanently blind. I have never been so scared in my life.

I know I'm the mom and so I'm supposed

to be strong and I'm really trying but oh, God, if something goes wrong.

We had a party for you, and all your friends came over. Nina and Claire and Kristen and Jake and even that poor little boy Lucas who lives up the hill. He seems so sad, although maybe I'm just projecting. The whole world seems sad to me right now. Your father blames himself, because he didn't want to take Benjamin to see a specialist earlier. The doctors have told him it wouldn't have made any

difference, but your father
blames himself for everything.
We've tried not to tell you
anything that will worry you,
but you're such a smart girl.
I've seen the way you've been so
sweet to Benjamin, doing all his
chores, bringing him cold cloths
when he gets those headaches. I
know you know something is
happening. I even know that
you're trying to keep up a brave
front and not let me know how
upset you are. In school
you wrote a poem about your
family. It's hard not to
think you wrote it to
reassure me, and I

guess yourself, too. Maybe I'm reading into it, but the part about everything being okay just broke my heart.

My Family

I am Zoey, and I am the smallest, My dad is the oldest, and also the tallest.

My big brother Benjamin's very cool, and often walks with me to school.

My mom is nice and always says yes, except sometimes when she has PMS.

We live on an island out in the bay,

and I am happy, I would say.

Even when things are sometimes sad, for me and Ben and my mom and my dad, I know everything will be okay, Because that's what my dad and my mom always say.

Your teacher says you're very gifted. You got an A-plus. Benjamin complained because you used "Ben." You know how he is about people shortening his name.

I guess the birthday party wasn't too much fun for you this year. I hope you'll understand later why we sometimes didn't give you all the attention you deserve right now.

At age ten you just amaze me by how graceful and grown up you are. Already the little boys, especially Jake, are giving you looks. Today at the party he shook up a bottle of Coke and sprayed you with it. I think it was a sign of affection.

Hopefully next year's birthday will be better. I'm optimistic.

Eight

The ferry pulled away from the dock at seven forty A.M., precise and on time as always. Fog hung still and low over the harbor, muffling the roar of the engines, yet paradoxically magnifying the churning gurgle of water as it rushed along the sides. During the night, clouds had moved in to hide the rising sun. It was as if they were all trapped inside a pearl, surrounded by shimmering translucence, unable to see farther than the deck.

The ferry sounded its foghorn as it rounded the breakwater and entered choppier water. Behind them the island had already disappeared. Ahead the mainland remained invisible.

Zoey wiped condensation from her forehead with the back of her sleeve.

"How does Skipper Too know where to drive the boat when it's like this?" Nina wondered aloud.

"Radar," Aisha said in a hushed voice.

"Or else just habit," Nina suggested. "He's done it a million times."

"Yeah, but how can he be sure there aren't other boats in the way?"

"We're bigger than they are. We just crush them."

Aisha shook her head emphatically. "Radar."

''Instinct,'' Nina said.

Aisha leaned forward to look past Zoey, making eye contact with Nina. ''Did Zoey fall into a coma and no one told us?''

''She's probably just thinking deep, profound thoughts,'' Nina said.

Zoey forced herself up out of her reverie. She couldn't leave Nina to defend her. Nina knew the truth now, but Nina was weak at keeping secrets. ''I just didn't sleep very well last night. I'm spacey.''

''Oh, come on, you're spacey every day,'' Aisha teased. ''Jeez, this fog is making my hair frizz.''

Zoey managed a wan smile. ''Radar,'' she said. ''Plus everyone who has a boat around here knows where the ferry is at any given time.''

''Told you she was thinking deep, profound thoughts,'' Nina said. ''Uh-oh.''

''Uh-oh, what?'' Aisha asked.

''A sad yet horny figure emerges from the fog.''

Zoey focused and saw Lucas coming toward them. She sighed inwardly, though there was at the same time a shadow of the familiar surge of warmth and excitement she always felt on seeing him. There was no point in avoiding him any longer. She got up heavily from the bench.

''Watch his hands,'' Nina whispered.

''Don't take any crap,'' Aisha advised. ''Make him beg.''

She met Lucas at the stern rail overlooking the wake. A pair of harbor seals floated contentedly, their sleek heads bobbing like buoys, watching the ferry pass with shrewd, intelligent eyes.

''Hi,'' Lucas said.

''Hi.''

He made an indeterminate gesture with his hands. "I thought maybe we should talk."

"Okay."

"I, uh . . . I think maybe I came on a little too strong. You know. When we were in Vermont."

Zoey said nothing.

"Okay, I came on way too strong. Look, I don't want to break up. You don't want to break up, do you?"

Zoey shook her head.

Lucas sighed in obvious relief.

For a while they were both silent. Zoey stared into the blankness of the fog. "I shouldn't have run away like that," she said at last. "That was stupid. But then, sometimes I'm just stupid."

Lucas looked surprised. "You've never been stupid, Zoey."

"About lots of things," she said. About lots of people. Naive and young and stupid.

"It was my fault," Lucas said.

Zoey was surprised. Lucas's fault? Oh, yes. That. She waved a hand. "Lots of stuff, not just that. It's just that sometimes things aren't what you think they are. People aren't *who* you think they are."

"Look, I said I'm sorry—"

Zoey shook her head. "No, I'm sorry. I'm just weird because I'm tired and because the sun's not out. I always get a little depressed when it's like this. Plus first day back at school after a long weekend."

Lucas slid his hand along the rail. He placed it over Zoey's. Zoey intertwined her fingers with his. It felt so familiar, yet like something she hadn't done in years. Still, there was a reassurance there. She wasn't surprised when he moved closer. When he put his other arm around her waist.

She was grateful for the warmth. Even now, as far-away as she was in her mind, his touch was comforting. If the last few days had been different, she would have been ecstatic that they were making up. She loved Lucas. She did. But that feeling had become overlain with darker feelings of more recent vintage.

His face was now close to hers. A face she loved, but one now strange to her. Yet his kiss was as soft and warm as ever. And she responded in the way she knew he wanted.

"You know when you said I wasn't acting very grown up?" she said when at last they had drawn apart.

He looked embarrassed. "I didn't really—"

"No. You were right about that," she said. "I've been a real child. A little girl."

Lucas seemed unable to come up with a response. He just looked uncomfortable.

Zoey smiled crookedly and squeezed his hand. "Never mind, Lucas. Not your problem."

Before first period Jake went to the gym. He had walked from the ferry landing up the street and then, as soon as he was out of sight of the others, he'd broken into an easy run, reaching school without breaking a sweat.

The coach was waiting in his office, a small, glass-walled area beside the equipment room. He looked up as Jake burst into the room, keeping his expression perfectly neutral.

"You ready to do this, McRoyan?"

"Yes, sir."

"You're sure? Because once I send off the sample, it's out of my hands."

"No problem," Jake said confidently.

The coach handed him a small plastic vial with a screw-on lid. "Don't need to fill more than half."

Jake took the bottle and went to the boys' locker room. When he was done he returned, feeling ridiculously self-conscious walking around with a little bottle of urine.

He set the bottle on the coach's desk. The coach nodded. "Kind of embarrassing, isn't it?"

"A little," Jake admitted.

"Good. You know I cut you slack on this, don't you?"

"Yes, sir."

"You're a good kid. Not a bad football player. I don't like to see a kid like you screw up the whole rest of his life by making one mistake."

Jake nodded. He felt strangely choked up. "Y'sir, Coach."

His coach stood up. He leaned across his desk, putting his face close to Jake's. "You've used up your freebie. You show up at any practice of mine, or any game of mine drunk, half-drunk, near-drunk, stoned, high, even thinking about being high, and you won't know what hit you. You'll be off the team. I'll let Mr. Hardcastle know what's happening. And I will personally go to your father and tell him. Do you read me?"

Jake nodded. "I understand."

"Well, you'd better." The coach shook his head regretfully. "What happened to your brother is not going to happen to another one of my players, or to another one of Fred McRoyan's sons."

Jake realized with horror that there were tears in his own eyes. It had never occurred to him that the coach might feel responsible in any way for Wade's drinking and death. When he answered, his voice was shaky. "No, sir."

"Okay, then. Be at practice tonight. And I am going to personally run your ass off. Now get out of here and we don't talk about this again."

Jake turned away, feeling both relief and a nagging worry. He stopped with his hand on the door. "Coach?"

"What now?"

"Zoey Passmore . . . She and I used to go out."

"Do I care?"

"She takes journalism and sometimes she writes for the *Weymouth Times*. You know, their youth page or whatever it's called."

"I'm still waiting to hear why I give a rat's ass."

Jake took a deep breath. "She says she's doing a story on rumors that there's drug use on the football team."

There was a long silence.

"What does she know?"

Jake shrugged. "I don't know. She asked me if I knew anything. I blew her off."

The coach gave him a long, cold stare. "Sounds like a personal problem, McRoyan."

Nine

Lucas had been right about the Department of Motor Vehicles, but it hadn't done Christopher any good. There were papers to fill out, and an ID he would have had to show, and some long story about filling out a police report on the alleged accident. None of which Christopher could do without leaving a huge, easy-to-read trail of evidence pointing straight to him.

Not that he was thinking that way, he reminded himself. That kind of thinking was for criminals. He was out for justice.

Instead, after getting off from his midday job as equipment manager for the school phys-ed department, he caught a city bus out to the part of town where he had spotted the skinheads in their car. He remembered the car. And he had the license number. And he had seen them turn down Brice Street, which, the map showed, dead-ended against the river after less than half a mile length.

He had slipped a box cutter into his pocket, a short metal handle that held an exposed razor blade. It wasn't much of a weapon, but if the people he was after should happen to spot him, at least he would have some means of defense.

He got off the bus, finding himself in a neighborhood of shabby homes and corner lots marked by self-serve gas stations and mini-marts. As he walked down Brice, the habitations became more spread out, separated by empty fields, by stands of pine, then clustered two or three together. A frame house with a trailer parked alongside. A kennel from which floated the plaintive cries of bored, hungry dogs. A rusted green mobile home with equally rusted appliances in the side yard and a hand-scrawled plywood sign offering rabbits for sale.

From time to time as he walked, Christopher caught sight of the river, brown and slow moving. He walked on the balls of his feet, fists unconsciously clenched in his jacket pockets. This was a world away from the urbane, relatively sophisticated heart of Weymouth, and farther still from the gentleness of Chatham Island. Here, while the environment was utterly different, the *feeling*, the mood, was closer to what he had known in the projects of Baltimore. There was sullen, lurking danger here, waiting like carelessly strewn explosives for the spark to set them off.

Then he spotted the car around a curve in the road, just a rear bumper protruding from the cover of trees. He stopped. In the low, slanting light it was hard to see clearly. In an hour it would be dark. In two hours he was due at the Passmores' restaurant to start the night shift.

An image of that familiar place, a gleaming, bright, stainless steel and tile kitchen, seemed like a vision from another planet. Here he was, creeping along the quiet road, his heart pounding, breath fast and rasping cold in his throat. Closer, closer.

Yes. The Ford. The correct numbers on the license plate.

He stepped over the ditch that ran beside the road and plunged into the scruffy pine woods. He circled, moving as silently as he could over pine needles, with thorn bushes snaring his ankles. Finally he crouched behind a tree, peering through a hole in the vegetation. He saw a frame house, not large, not painted in many years. A bare window. A woman standing there, head down, shoulders moving slightly. Washing dishes in her kitchen sink, Christopher realized.

He checked his watch. Not much time left if he was to make work on time. Now that he was standing still, he felt the cold. He had to pee urgently. A dog on a long chain walked by in the side yard of the house. It stopped and stared, ears cocked exactly at the spot where Christopher was standing.

Christopher froze. After an eternity the dog walked away toward the backyard.

In the window another figure, passing by behind the woman. Just a glimpse of a bare head reflecting harsh light, a short goatee.

A second window was illuminated. Christopher shifted his position slightly. And there it was, hanging loosely on a wall. Red, white, and blue in an *X* of stars—the Confederate battle flag.

Christopher nodded grimly. Maybe—*maybe*—if this had been the South, that flag might have stood for some twisted notion of local history. But this was Maine. As Yankee as a state could be. Here the stars and bars could only be the symbol of racism.

The shaved head and goatee stopped in front of the window.

Yes, Christopher told himself, that was him. That was one of the creatures who had beaten him, knocked him to the dirty ground, kicked and kicked and kicked . . .

Christopher pointed a finger at the unseeing boy inside. Pointed a finger and silently mouthed the word *bang*.

Ten

Zoey reached into her desk drawer for an eraser and realized with a shock that there was an unfamiliar empty space there. The journal. It had been in that drawer forever.

She glanced at her trash can. But no, she remembered now. She had taken out the trash last night. The journal, with all her writing, and the book her mother had given her. Gone now. No point having second thoughts. They were both artifacts from a time in her life that was over.

She erased the error she'd made on her trig homework, wrote in the correct answer, and rechecked her calculation. Yes. That was right. Or at least it seemed right. Math of any kind was not her strongest subject. Tomorrow morning on the ferry she'd check with Aisha. Aisha was taking calculus and regularly complained that the class moved too slowly.

There was a knock on her bedroom door. "It's me." Lucas's voice.

Zoey hesitated. "Come in."

Lucas was wearing a rough oversized sweater that made him look smaller than he was. Not quite vulnerable, that would be overstating it, but adorable. His long blond hair was windblown, his cheeks pink from the cold outside. His lips were a little chapped.

He came and stood behind her and rested his hands on her shoulders, looking down at her work. "Homework?" he asked.

"I'm all done," she said. "I just finished." She could sense his hesitation. He wanted to kiss her, but there was still an uncertainty between them, no doubt made worse by Zoey's preoccupation with other matters. Matters like the two still-unread letters under the edge of her mattress.

She felt his lips on the top of her head. She tilted back, raising her face to him, closing her eyes. Yes, his lips were a little chapped, and his hand, stroking her cheek, was cold.

She broke free and stood up, intending to continue kissing him from a more comfortable position. But he was staring at the walls of her dormered window.

"What happened to all your quotes?"

She shrugged nonchalantly, but she was aware that a blush would soon be appearing on her face. She had forgotten that others might notice a difference in her room. "I don't know. Decided it was time for a change."

"Oh." He nodded. "I liked them. Always had something new to think about whenever I came up here."

"You always think about exactly the same thing whenever you're up here," Zoey said, hoping to distract him.

He made a wry smile. "I think about that everywhere, not just here. But I liked that quote about school. About it being unhappy and dull . . . what was it again?"

Zoey picked up her *Portable Curmudgeon* and flipped to the page. She held it out for Lucas.

" 'School days, I believe, are the unhappiest in the whole span of human existence. They are full of dull, unintelligible tasks, new and unpleasant ordinances, brutal violations of common sense and common decency.' " Lucas laughed delightedly. "H. L. Mencken, I don't know who you were, but you're my man. 'Dull, unintelligible tasks.' Think he attended Weymouth High?"

There was a louder knock at the door. A deep male voice. "All right, break clean in there."

"Come in, Daddy," Zoey said quickly.

Lucas shot her a mildly disgruntled look.

"Lucas!" Mr. Passmore said in mock surprise. "Imagine finding you here."

"What's up, Mr. P.?"

"Have I mentioned that you can call me Jeff?"

"Yes, sir," Lucas said.

"But I'm way too old for you to call by my first name, right?" Her father winced and sent Zoey a droll look. "I just wanted to see if you guys wanted to come down and watch TV. *Drew Carey* is on in a few minutes. And I feel like I haven't seen you much lately, between work and you going off for the weekend."

Zoey hurried to her father's side. "I'll come watch TV with you. Come on, Lucas."

"We'll do popcorn," Mr. Passmore said, enticing Lucas, making up for the fact that he was depriving Lucas of his girlfriend.

"And beer?" Lucas asked, giving way gracefully.

"Don't mind if I do," Mr. Passmore said. "And of course there are soft drinks for you."

They trotted downstairs, joining Benjamin and Nina in the family room. Benjamin and Nina were close together on the couch, hands intertwined. Lucas pulled Zoey down beside him on the love seat, and Zoey's father flopped back in the La-Z-Boy.

"Well," Mr. Passmore said with a wistful smile, "I'm the only one without a date."

After Nina and Lucas had gone home, Benjamin and Zoey stayed with their father. They watched some more TV together, and during commercial breaks that Mr. Passmore muted with the remote control, they exchanged brief bits of conversation.

Zoey was sitting on the couch, leaning back against the armrest with her legs up and covered by a throw. Her father was in profile, focused on the TV. His usual ponytail was unfastened so that his dark hair hung loose, not quite reaching his shoulders. At the front his hairline had started to recede. He wore a nondescript gray T-shirt and an old pair of painter's pants and heavy wool socks on his feet. He was drinking a Bass from the bottle and scrounging for the remnants of popcorn in a glass bowl.

Did he know? Zoey wondered. Did he at least suspect?

Did he sense the seismic forces building up beneath him, waiting to bring down his world?

"Glad Christopher's on the job again," he said, muting a car commercial. "It's nice to be able to kick back a little."

"He's probably glad to be back at work, too," Zoey said.

"He works hard. Man, when I was his age I only worked till I could afford my next set of Dead tickets and gas money to get there."

Zoey smiled affectionately. "Do you ever think of doing that again? I mean, the Grateful Dead are still around."

Her father laughed. ''Yeah, I think about it. Although nowadays I think about maybe getting a room at a nearby Marriott instead of sleeping in the back of a van or in a field somewhere.'' He shrugged. ''I don't know if your mom would be up for it, either.''

Zoey became alert. ''Did you guys used to do stuff like that?''

''You mean back when we had lives?'' he asked dryly. ''Sure.''

''What do you mean 'when we had lives'?'' Zoey asked. She didn't want to sound like she was pumping him for information, but she was.

''Before they had us,'' Benjamin interjected.

''No, it was more the restaurant,'' Mr. Passmore said. ''Since we got that, we haven't had time for much. I feel like I barely see your mom, except at work. And I don't see much of you two, either.''

He put the sound back on the TV and they listened to a local news story about a bus wreck.

''When did you guys decide to get married?'' Zoey asked.

She noticed Benjamin cocking an eyebrow quizzically. ''Right after they found out Mom was pregnant with me,'' he said.

''Very funny, Benjamin,'' Mr. Passmore said.

''Yeah, and true. I can count, you know.''

This wasn't a big surprise to Zoey. She and Benjamin had figured out this titillating bit of information years ago. Their parents' anniversary came three months after Benjamin would have been conceived. ''Was Mom your only girlfriend?''

Zoey's father gave her a surprised look. ''What is this, Twenty Questions?''

''I was just curious.''

For a fleeting moment her father's eyes grew vacant, faraway. But then, just as quickly, he shook off the passing mood. He covered it by affecting a swaggering tone. "I wasn't totally unpopular with the young ladies."

"Anyone special?"

Benjamin was doing the subtle tilt of the head that was his version of staring. He was concentrating on Zoey, a quizzical smile tugging at the corners of his mouth. She was going to have to stop this questioning or Benjamin's suspicions would be fully alerted.

"Special?" her father repeated the word. He shrugged. "Nah. Not really. Just your mom. She was the one who had guys after her all the time."

"At the same time she was going out with you?"

Her father turned the La-Z-Boy and looked at her. "Oh, no you don't. You can't use your mom and me as guides for how you deal with Lucas. Do as we say, not as we did."

Zoey formed a sheepish smile.

"But—now don't tell your mom this—but I do think she had some other guy going at the same time as me."

Zoey nearly gave it away, but fought to maintain control of her features. Her voice wobbled a little, but she plowed on, hoping her father wouldn't notice. It was Benjamin, she knew, who wouldn't miss her emotion. "Another guy, huh?"

"Some jock or marine or something. So I heard. Never knew the guy's name. It was while I was away for a time. Backpacking around Europe while your mom was still in school." He smiled wistfully. "Fortunately for me, it all worked out, huh? I don't know what I would have done if she hadn't been in my life."

To my daughter,

Well. Didn't you get an odd present for your twelfth birthday? Two days ago you came to me, very adult and ladylike, and said, "Mother, I believe I have started my period." I knew it was something major as soon as you said "Mother" because you never call me that.

You handled it so much better than I did when it happened to me. With me there was crying. But then, my mother never was good at telling me all the facts of life, whereas we've always tried to be honest with you. I remember when you were five you asked us how babies are made and your dad found an excuse to leave the room, so I had to tell you.

Anyway, I was very proud of how grown up you were the other day. Your dad became depressed, of course, because to him it means you're growing up, which means he's growing older. Also, he's so nuts about you, and he doesn't want you to turn into a teenager. He probably remembers what we were both like as teenagers. And for that matter after we were teenagers.

I guess this means you've made the first big step from being a girl to being a woman. I know you'll be a wonderful woman because you've always been such a great kid. This last year you've had to deal with Benjamin and his therapy still taking everyone's attention away from you. Not to mention that Nina and Claire's mom died and that has hurt you terribly.

I hope you'll do a better job with your life than I have in

some ways with mine. Maybe I can help you make fewer mistakes because I've definitely made some. Not that I'm ever going to tell you about them. I wouldn't want to give you any ideas. Soon you'll be a teenager and then you and I will probably have trouble. Most teen girls have hassles with their moms. God knows I did. I think it's when you're a teenager that you start to realize that your parents don't actually know everything. But I hope you and I can beat the odds and go on

being close, because I love you.
Even if you weren't my
daughter I would think you
were pretty cool.

Eleven

Zoey's room, 6:31 A.M.

The radio alarm went off a minute late. For a moment Zoey was confused. The song on the radio was from one of her favorite albums. She recognized the Jewel lyrics immediately.

It was like a message. An omen. The message was grim but strong. She would do whatever she had to do. Whatever it took to make sense . . . in the ruins.

One thing had become clear as crystal last night—the first and most important thing to do was protect her father. He was the innocent person in all this and he was the one who would be hurt the worst.

It's so clear now, she thought as she quickly dressed. As if the last of the confusion had been left behind in her dreams. Now she knew exactly what to do. She hefted her books, slung her purse over her shoulder, and headed for the door. Then she went back to her bed, bent down, and removed the letters from under her mattress. The last thing she needed if she was going to succeed was for her mother to find the letters.

Camden Street, 7:32 A.M.

Benjamin walked at her side, moving along the familiar path to the ferry like a sighted person. Except that Zoey knew in his head he was counting, making each step as nearly identical as possible, and keeping track on some subliminal level of all the tiny clues that only he noticed—the interval of coolness and warmth that was the sun peeking between gaps in the houses; the welcoming good-morning bark of the Brashares' big Labrador, Danny; the smell of the fresh doughnuts frying that meant they were passing Island Grocery.

"Sunny today?" Benjamin asked.

"Mostly," Zoey said. Her mind was still on her mission. It would take courage.

Benjamin grumbled good-naturedly. "That's one of the things I miss about going out with Claire," he said. "You ask her about the weather, you get a full, complete answer."

Claire Geiger had a somewhat strange obsession with weather, up to the point of sitting out in the middle of thunderstorms from atop her widow's walk.

"So," he said.

"So what?"

"So, you going to tell me why you were giving the old man the treatment last night?"

"What treatment?"

"Like you were interviewing him to see if he should be a contestant on *Singled Out*."

"I was just curious. I mean, he's our dad, but how much do we really know about him?"

This struck Benjamin as very funny, fortunately for Zoey. "Yeah, who knows what dark secrets the old man is hiding?"

"There's Nina up ahead."

Benjamin accelerated, caught his toe in a sidewalk brick, and barely kept from tripping.

Zoey snickered.

"That was not because I was excited about seeing Nina or anything," he said gruffly.

"Uh-huh."

The ferry, 7:48 A.M.

From across the deck of the ferry, Jake was watching her. Obviously something was bothering him. She hoped it wasn't what she feared it was. She didn't see any way he could possibly know. But secrets were hard to keep on an island as small as Chatham Island.

She squeezed out from between Nina and Aisha, who were arguing over whether Marilyn Manson was cool or full of himself. Lucas was against the far railing. When he saw her get up, he started toward her with a smile on his face. But then, realizing she was going to Jake, he backed off, his expression coldly mistrustful.

"Hi, Jake," she said.

"Hey, Zoey," he said guardedly.

"You're not sitting with Claire?" she asked, by way of making conversation. She wanted him to have a chance to bring up whatever was bugging him. She wanted to hear him first, decide what he knew before committing herself.

"She's busy reading," Jake said, sounding mildly annoyed. "Sometimes I get the feeling I may not be the center of her existence."

"Claire is the sun and moon in her very own solar system," Zoey said.

He made a half-smile. "So. How's the big story going?"

"The big story?" Good grief, she'd practically forgotten. Mr. Schwarz, her journalism teacher, would kill her if she blew it. "I haven't had any time to work on it."

He nodded. He was looking at her through narrowed slits. Skeptical. "What are you going to do next? You know, on the story."

She shrugged. "I guess I'll talk to some of the other guys on the team."

"I doubt if anyone will have anything to say."

"Maybe not. Um, Jake, are you pissed off at me?"

"Why would I be?"

"I don't know."

"No, Zoey. I don't have a problem with you." Belligerent.

"Okay. And . . . and you don't have a problem with Benjamin, or anyone else in my family?" She tried out a lighthearted tone.

He looked quizzical. "What?"

"Nothing."

Journalism class, first period

As she was on her way out, Mr. Schwarz beckoned to her. She sighed and went over by his desk. Mr. Schwarz was the best-looking male teacher in the school, but when he was impatient or annoyed with someone, he tended not to look quite as cute.

"Getting anywhere with that story I gave you to do?" he asked, crossing his arms over his chest.

"Not yet," Zoey admitted. "Although I asked my friend, my source, you know, the guy I said I knew who's on the team?"

''Jake McRoyan,'' Mr. Schwarz said.

''Uh-huh,'' Zoey admitted. Somehow mentioning Jake by name had seemed indiscreet. It made it too personal and unprofessional. ''He says no way. He says he would know.''

Mr. Schwarz stared at her. Then he took a deep breath. ''Keep digging, Zoey.''

''I was going to talk to some of the other guys on the team.''

''Good idea. You might also try checking to see who on the team may have missed games or turned in a poor performance lately.''

''That's a good idea,'' Zoey said. She glanced at the clock. It would be a run to make trig.

''Okay. Go,'' Mr. Schwarz said, dismissing her and looking cuter again for a moment.

Good ideas, Zoey thought admiringly. *Check on who had missed a game recently*. Too bad she'd been out of town over the weekend. So she hadn't seen the game.

And, of course, neither had Jake.

Jake?

No. Impossible.

Except that the week before at homecoming, Jake had seemed . . . *No. Not Jake,* Zoey thought, trying to dismiss the idea.

But if it *was* him—if Jake *was* the person who had been using drugs . . .

She groaned. Like life wasn't complicated enough right now?

Twelve

"You know, I'm seventeen," Aisha said. "I'll be graduating soon. Off to college. And my point is, I don't think I'll suddenly decide at this time in my life to become a gymnast." She adjusted the water to be a little warmer and rotated slowly so that the shower could rinse the soap from her body. "Tell me why I would want to risk breaking my neck vaulting."

"You could be the next what's-her-name," Zoey said, stepping out of the water gingerly and running on tiptoes to her towel.

"She could be the next three-foot-tall anorexic?" Claire asked archly. "I doubt it."

"What are you talking about?" Zoey asked.

"Gymnasts. They're all the size of munchkins and eat nothing but rice cakes."

"Exactly," Aisha said, turning off the water. She buried her face in her towel. "So why are we doing gymnastics?"

"Why are we doing any of this?" Claire demanded. "Because the school district says we have to and we didn't get it out of the way last year like we should have."

"Do you guys realize you have this same conversation every day?'' asked Louise Kronenberger as she slipped on a sweater.

''We find it comforting,'' Claire said.

''Maybe we should try to get into it more,'' Louise suggested. ''Like the guys do.''

''They're in their locker room snapping each other with towels right now,'' Claire said. ''Is that what you think we should be doing?''

Louise got a dreamy, faraway look in her eyes. ''No. But you've drawn a nice word picture, Claire. It conjures up some interesting mental images. Does Jake have gym this period?'' she asked innocently.

''I don't think you want to be imagining Jake,'' Aisha warned. ''They're back together.''

Louise grinned. ''But it's so easy for me to imagine Jake.'' She batted her eyes. ''I can even imagine a crooked little scar right . . . but then, I'm letting my imagination run wild.'' She looked in the mirror, patted her hair, and gave a good-bye wave.

Aisha noted the sudden narrowing of Claire's eyes, but she instantly regained control. The girl was cool, there was no question about that. But of course Claire knew there had never been anything between Louise and Jake. At least, Aisha was pretty sure there had never been anything between Jake and Louise. That would be hard to imagine. Jake was the last of the major straight arrows, and Louise . . .

Aisha finished dressing and went outside, skirting the edge of the polished gym floor. Christopher worked in the equipment room and it wouldn't hurt to stop by and say hello, since she had a few minutes.

The equipment room was a dark, not exactly fragrant place with metal shelves lined with things like volleyball nets, tumbling mats, jumbled piles of white plastic football pads, racks of baseball bats, and every type of ball known to man or woman.

Christopher had a clipboard in one hand, a pencil in the other, and earphones over his ears. He was intent on counting and hadn't noticed her.

Aisha crept up behind him and slid her arms around his waist. He jerked at first, but then relaxed without turning around. She kissed the back of his neck. He pulled off the earphones.

"Is that you, Natalie?"

Aisha slapped him on the arm. He spun around.

"I was kidding. Just kidding." He rubbed the spot.

"I knew you were kidding."

"Then why did you nearly bruise me?"

"Because I'm sure you've done something to deserve it," Aisha replied. "What are you doing?"

"While I was off, it seems a certain amount of equipment managed to disappear. Three basketballs, a catcher's mask, and a croquet set."

"Croquet set? Why do we have a croquet set?"

He shrugged. "Why do we have six bowling balls and a jigsaw puzzle of a cat playing with a ball of yarn? It's not my job to ask why. I just keep track of the stuff and keep it in shape."

"Well, I guess I'd better get going," Aisha said.

"Where to?"

"Homeroom, then lunch." Aisha considered an idea that had popped into her mind, rejected it, considered it again, and rejected it again. Then she went ahead and said it anyway. "You know, if you ever wanted to have lunch together—"

"Don't you eat in the cafeteria with the other females of the Chatham Island club?"

"Usually. But there's no law saying I have to. We

are allowed off-campus, you know, and there's Burger King and the Dashing Deli."

"The deli's all right," he said. "We use their rolls at the restaurant. Mr. Passmore says they're the best bakery around. I'd love to have lunch with you there, Aisha. I wish I'd thought of it. How about tomorrow?"

"Why not today? It's Wok Wednesday in the cafeteria. They pretend it's Chinese food except that I don't think there's anything very Chinese about cut-up pieces of Salisbury steak mixed with bean sprouts."

Christopher winced. "Can't do it today," he said.

"You have to eat," Aisha pointed out. "You do get a lunch hour, don't you?"

"Yes," he said. Then he glanced away. "Only today I have to do something else." He looked down at his clipboard.

"Fine," Aisha said. "I can take the hint."

"Wait." He grabbed her arm. "I'd really, really like to take you to lunch tomorrow."

"I'll check my schedule," Aisha said. *And maybe*, she added to herself, *I'll just check out what you* are *doing during lunch today.*

"So where's Aisha?" Nina asked, taking the seat across from Claire and next to Zoey. She set down her tray and took a long look at what the cafeteria ladies had given her.

Claire shrugged indifferently. "Not my day to keep track of Aisha." In about ten seconds Nina would come up with something gross to say about the food. Ten, nine, eight . . .

"I don't know, either," Zoey said.

. . . seven, six . . .

''Wait! Someone barfed on my tray,'' Nina said, wrinkling her nose.

Four seconds to spare. ''Every day,'' Claire said wearily.

''Every day what?''

''Every day you have to say something disgusting about the disgusting food.''

''I don't have to,'' Nina argued. ''It's just that they make it so easy. I mean, you know what this stuff looks like?''

''Please don't tell me,'' Claire said, knowing full well that nothing short of an anvil dropped from a great height directly on Nina's head would stop her.

''Like what's left after someone's been dead for a month and the worms have gotten to them.''

Zoey pushed away her food. Nina gleefully took a big bite. Claire forked up a bite of hers, giving Nina a defiant look.

''Why don't you go sit with Benjamin?'' Claire asked. ''I'm sure he'd appreciate your descriptive talents.''

''I didn't want to mess with tradition,'' Nina said airily. ''We always sit together. Although without Aisha it kind of changes the balance a little. Basically, it means too much of you.''

''Maybe *I* should go sit with Benjamin,'' Claire said, sending a long look from under lowered lashes in his direction. ''That shirt looks good on him. Did you pick that out for him, Zoey?''

Zoey did a snap back to reality. ''What? Oh, yeah. You know, the guys' store that's next to Express at the mall?''

''Maybe I *should* go over and say hi,'' Nina said, standing up with her tray. ''Since Aisha isn't here and Zoey's obviously off in the ozone, anyway.''

Claire allowed herself a small smile of satisfaction. Unfortunately, Nina's description of the main course had had an effect. She ate her bread and apple and drank her juice.

"Can I ask you a question?" Zoey asked suddenly, breaking in on Claire's contented silence.

"Go ahead."

"Do you think Jake ever used any drugs?"

Claire came fully alert. Jake had told her about his one nearly disastrous encounter with drugs. And of course she knew all about Jake's drinking—more than the one or two occasions Zoey and the others knew about. "Jake?" she said, sounding incredulous. "Why would you think that?"

Zoey looked thoughtful. "You know how sometimes I write stories for the youth page of the *Weymouth Times*?"

Claire nodded.

"They asked me to check out rumors that there's a drug problem on the football team."

Claire let loose a stream of silent curses. But outwardly she showed nothing. Or at least she hoped she showed nothing. Zoey wasn't stupid.

"So I asked Jake about it when we were up in Vermont and he got all pissed off."

"He's loyal to his teammates," Claire said.

"That's what I thought, too. But then I started thinking about how he missed the game last weekend."

"He went with us to Vermont."

"The game was on Friday night. We left on Saturday morning."

Claire finished chewing a bit of apple. There was an "official" story for why Jake hadn't played that game. But Zoey wasn't going to buy it for a minute.

Still, it was the only story Claire had available. "He said something about a pulled muscle."

Zoey shook her head. "He was skiing all weekend. Skiing hard, too."

Claire concentrated again on her apple. Well, it had been worth a try. Now she wished she hadn't manipulated Nina into leaving. Zoey might not have brought all this up with Nina around.

Zoey leaned forward and pitched her voice at an intimate level. "Look, Claire, I think maybe those rumors are actually about Jake."

She could deny, or pretend to be indifferent, or she could tell Zoey the truth and try to get her to drop it. And the longer she hesitated indecisively, the more suspicious Zoey would become. "I don't think this is any of my business," she said at last.

"You're going out with Jake, Claire. If he's been doing drugs, that has to be your business."

"What exactly do you want from me?" Claire snapped. "You want me to help you write your little story?"

"God, it *is* him," Zoey said. She covered her mouth with her hand.

"I didn't say that."

"I wish someone had told me before I agreed to do this thing," Zoey said.

Claire gave up. There was no point in denying it now. Zoey knew. "It was just the one time, Zoey. They suspended him from the team for a week until he could pass a urinalysis, which he did yesterday. That's really not much of a story, is it?"

"Is he okay?"

"Do you care if he's okay?"

"Of course I do," Zoey said. "I still care about Jake. We were together a long time."

She was obviously sincere. Perhaps a little too sincere, Claire decided. Things must not be total perfection between Zoey and Lucas. ''If you care about Jake, then drop it. He knows sooner or later some of the people here will find out about it, but you know how he is with his father. If his father ever found out, Jake would feel like the lowest form of garbage.''

''His father.'' Zoey nodded grimly. ''He cares too much what his father thinks about him.''

''People usually do.''

''Do you?'' Zoey asked sharply. ''I mean, do you really care that much what your father thinks?''

The question made Claire uncomfortable. What did this have to do with Jake? ''I suppose I do.''

Zoey nodded. ''Parents are just people, you know.''

''I had heard that somewhere,'' Claire answered dryly. ''What are you going to do about this story?''

Zoey's eyes flickered. She had been off somewhere, thinking about something else. ''I don't know. I don't want to hurt Jake. It's important to me that he doesn't get hurt. He's part of the reason why—''

''Why what?''

Zoey made a forced smile. ''Never mind. I'll have to think about it.''

Aisha waited just inside a glass-windowed side door to the school. From here she could see the gym doors. Dozens of students were passing across her field of vision, but she was sure she'd notice Christopher if he came by. She didn't wait long to spot his tall, lithe form, moving quickly to slide between slower-moving groups.

Aisha opened the door and went after him. There wasn't much likelihood that he would notice her. Christopher always walked and moved like he was on an urgent mission. The problem was keeping him in sight. Several times she had to break into a trot.

He left the campus and headed down the street, past the Burger King, where most of the rest of the crowd veered off. Christopher kept moving until he was well into the downtown business area, crossing the commons, teeming with lunching secretaries and young executives. He went down Fifth Street, plunging into a grubby neighborhood of row houses fronted by overflowing trash cans and decorated with spray-painted graffiti.

Aisha began feeling conspicuous, no longer shielded from his view if he should happen to turn around. Plus, she was beginning to realize that she would have a very hard time explaining this bit of spying to Christopher.

He slowed, seemed to be checking a street sign, and ducked into an alley.

Aisha hesitated. Maybe he had spotted her and was waiting just within the alley to jump out and yell "Aha!" And really, she was way, way past the point where she could try to pretend it was just a chance encounter. She'd never been on this street before, didn't know anyone here, had no conceivable excuse for being here.

Except for the excuse that she was spying on Christopher. Trying to find out why he hadn't wanted to have lunch with her. Frankly, she'd expected to find him sharing a chicken salad with some little bimbo he'd met. She certainly hadn't expected him to go this far from school. And if he was meeting another girl, this was an odd place to do it.

She went ahead, walking as inconspicuously as possible to the mouth of the alley. When she reached it, she sidled against the wall and looked around the corner with a motion that reminded her of a Bugs Bunny cartoon and made her feel like a complete idiot.

She jerked back her head. Christopher was only ten feet or so away, standing close to a twentysomething white guy with long sideburns.

She could hear snatches of a low, muttered conversation. Christopher's voice. "... serial number or anything?"

"That's all ... totally clean."

"Two bills?"

"... fifty."

"And you'll throw in ..." Christopher.

"Two fifty ... and a box of ... points."

Aisha strained. The sound of her own heart pounding in her ears was making it hard to hear.

Then she heard a sound with perfect clarity. A harsh metallic sound. Then a click. "That's all there is to it."

"Here's ... money."

"Cool ..."

"... never seen me." Christopher's voice.

A laugh. "Never seen anybody, my ..."

Aisha realized she had stopped breathing. For a moment she was paralyzed. The deal had been concluded. Christopher would be stepping out of the alley any second.

The sound of footsteps. She bolted, racing around the back of a car and crouching down below the windows. Looking left, she saw sideburns, hands shoved deep in his pockets, shoulders hunched. Then, in the other direction, Christopher. One hand was in the pocket of his coat, and the coat sagged on that side.

Aisha stood up. She was trembling. It was impossible not to know what had happened. At first Aisha had told herself Christopher was buying drugs. The truth was so terrible that even that would have been a relief. But there was no question. Christopher had bought a gun.

My dearest Darla—

I am so sorry for the way I reacted when you told me your news. I was angry and hurt but I shouldn't have yelled like I did. I guess I was afraid it would mean I would lose you and I don't want that to happen.

You said it couldn't be mine, that the timing doesn't work out. But it could be mine, if you agreed. No one would ever have to know. We could get married right away, before I get shipped out. That way you'd get what they call an allotment, part of my pay. Also, you could have the baby in a military hospital for free.

I swear to you, Darla, I would raise the child and love it like my own. It would be my own as far as anyone would ever be concerned. I don't want you to get an abortion just because you don't think the baby would have a father. And I also don't want you to leave me and go back to Jeff because of this.

I know we can work something out if you'll give it a chance. I'll be out of the army in three years. We could move to this great place I know called Chatham Island. It's a little island in Maine, a perfect place for raising kids and having a family. My own family lives near there, so I know people there and it's a great area.

Anyway, please think about it. I love you and will do anything to keep you.

Yours forever,

Fred

Thirteen

Zoey had never before skipped school, but so far, it was proving much easier than she'd imagined.

First, she'd had to come up with a plausible story for Lucas. Lucas was in her sixth-period history class *and* her last-period French. They always walked from the one to the other together. There was no possibility whatsoever that he would somehow not notice her absence. None.

So she'd told him that she had gotten permission to leave early and work on her journalism project. He'd seemed puzzled, but the last thing she could worry about at this crucial moment was Lucas.

The time had come, and now that it had, it filled her with dread. What she was preparing to do was unthinkable. Except that she had to think about it and plan it out. How she would explain why she was there in his office. What she would say. How she would deal with his possible denial. What specific words she would use. Adultery? Betrayal? No. She was going to keep everything very cool and adult and simply tell him that he must never again . . .

What? God, it was impossible even to imagine discussing any of this. It was insane.

Feeling guilty, Zoey headed down the empty hall

toward a side door. She had to ditch, she reminded herself. After school her plan would be impossible, with Nina and Benjamin and Aisha around. Besides, Mr. McRoyan might have left his work by then. And his work was the safest place to go to him.

Just at the door Ms. Lambert, her homeroom teacher, stepped out of a classroom.

Zoey froze. Her first attempt to skip school and she'd been busted!

But Ms. Lambert just smiled. "How are you, Zoey?"

"Fine," Zoey squeaked.

"See you tomorrow."

"Okay."

She was out the door. It was amazing what a spotless reputation could do for you. No one would ever suspect her of skipping school, so even on seeing Zoey brazenly walking out, the teacher had assumed she must have a good reason.

Zoey breathed a sigh of relief. Still, getting out of school was going to be the easy part.

She headed downtown, quiet now with all the worker bees back in their hives till the big five o'clock rush to freedom.

Mid-Maine Bank owned the tallest building in downtown, fifteen floors. Mr. Geiger's office on the top floor had a terrific view of the entire city. Zoey had gone up there several times with Nina or Claire. The lower floors were rented to a wide variety of businesses.

Zoey went in through the green-marbled lobby to the brass elevator. Her heart was in her throat as she pushed the button, and she knew that when it came to the actual moment, she would never be able to stay as cool as she hoped.

The elevator bell dinged and she got off on the fourth floor.

The silent, carpeted hallway was lined with wood doors, each marked with the name of the company or person that rented the individual offices—WEYMOUTH SAIL; DR. OSCAR BRILL, OPTOMETRIST; VISITING NURSE ASSOCIATION OF WEYMOUTH.

Zoey stopped at the door she was searching for.

She gritted her teeth. Her hands were sweaty, and she wiped them on her pants. Once through the door, she couldn't turn back. He would know why she had come. There would be no denying anything.

She put her hand on the knob, turned it, and stepped into the comfortable, modern offices of McRoyan Realty Holdings.

The receptionist looked up at her with a quizzical half-smile.

Zoey stared past her into the glass-walled office beyond.

It took several seconds for him to see Zoey, during which time the receptionist asked repeatedly why she was there, did she have an appointment, was she sure she was in the right place.

Fred McRoyan stood up slowly, levering himself up out of his chair, an older, heavier, but still-fit version of Jake. He stuck his head out of his office. "I'll see her, Ellen."

Zoey walked on stiff legs past the receptionist, blood rushing in her ears, breath rickety.

Mr. McRoyan closed his door behind her. "Would you like something to drink, Zoey? A soda? Coffee?"

"No, thank you."

He accepted that and went to sit behind his desk.

"Please . . ." He motioned to a chair.

She barely knew whether she had sat down or not.

He rubbed his face with both hands, then folded them before him.

So much like Jake, Zoey realized. Had she ever noticed it so intensely before? It was like seeing the future—Jake in twenty years.

And nothing at all like Benjamin. No, there was no similarity there at all.

"What can I do for you, Zoey?" he asked.

Zoey took a deep breath. "I wanted to talk to you."

"Okay."

Here it was. "I want you to leave us alone."

He said nothing, just looked at her, or past her; it was hard to tell.

"I saw you the other day," she said. "With my mom."

He nodded. "I thought maybe you had."

"Well, I did."

"You weren't supposed to be there," he said regretfully.

"*I* wasn't . . . *You* weren't supposed to be there! Me? It's my house. I'm supposed to be there, not *you*." Her face was hot. Her fists were clenched.

"You're right." He held up two placating hands. "I expressed that the wrong way."

Zoey let out a curse that shocked her.

Mr. McRoyan pressed his lips into a tight line. "Zoey, would it help if I told you it was just that one time?"

"That's bad enough." She wasn't going to tell him about the letters. She had read them all now. She knew about his past, and her mother's.

"Yes, it is. I am terribly sorry that you walked in on that."

"Sorry you got caught, you mean."

"Sorry I have made you feel badly toward your

mother. Your mother is a very fine woman."

Zoey sneered. "Yeah. Wonderful. Just stay away from all of us." She got up, intending to leave.

"I was in love with your mother."

She sat down again. So. He was going to tell the truth.

"A long time ago. She was still in college. I was in the army. Jump school. She had been seeing your dad, but he went off to Europe for a while to backpack and explore, I guess. Your mother and I—" He shrugged. "But I was on my way into the army and your dad came back. Anyway, that was that."

"Not quite."

"We never let anyone know. We've never so much as spoken of those days since you all came to live on the island. Then I guess something happened to make your mom feel . . ." He waved a hand. "Never mind. That's not the point. What I did was dead wrong and I am sorry."

That was it. He wasn't saying more. Zoey stood up again. "Just stay away from us. I don't want my dad to be hurt."

"I know."

"Good."

"Have you . . . Does Jake . . ."

"No," Zoey said shortly. "He's the other person I don't want to be hurt."

"Agreed." He stood up. "I know this won't mean much to you, Zoey, but I've always thought the world of you. I was sorry you and Jake didn't stay together."

"Good-bye," Zoey said. She wasn't sure what else to say. She looked at Mr. McRoyan's downcast face. He looked sincere. Maybe this really could be the end of it all.

But then his expression changed. His eyes widened. It was as if his whole person collapsed. It was like those slow-motion films of buildings that were being demolished. A shudder, and all at once all the strength went out of him.

Zoey turned and, staring through the glass partition, saw Jake.

Jake stared at the scene before him. Zoey, looking startled. His father looking as if he'd learned the worst news of his life.

Zoey had done it. She had gone to his father to ask him whether he knew that his son was accused of using drugs. It was the only possible explanation.

Why? Why would she do something like this? For some stupid story? It was unimaginable that Zoey, of all people . . .

His father covered his face with his hands, leaning his elbows on his desk. Zoey came out, closing his office door carefully. She looked down as she came to him.

Jake grabbed her arm roughly and pulled her out, past the receptionist into the silent hallway outside. She didn't resist.

"What were you doing in there?" he demanded, almost frantic. If his father knew, he would be devastated. He would think Jake was on his way to becoming Wade. He would imagine the worst. He would lose all faith in Jake, and if that happened, Jake didn't know what he would do.

"I had to talk to your father," Zoey said stiffly.

"You didn't have to!" Jake cried.

"I had to protect my family," Zoey said. Her eyes were blazing now.

"Your family." Jake felt he must have missed

something. Or else he was just stupidly failing to understand. What did his being suspended from the team have to do with Zoey's family?

"*And* yours," Zoey added.

"My family?"

"Yes. What happened was just about your father and my mother. It shouldn't break up our families. My dad still loves my mother, I know he does. I can tell, the way he talks about her. And I know he'd . . . It would destroy him."

Zoey was just rambling, staring blankly past Jake, almost as if she were thinking out loud. She was justifying something, explaining something to herself.

Jake shook his head in frustration. "What did my dad say?"

"He said he wouldn't let it happen again," Zoey answered. Then she peered at him, as though noticing him for the first time. "I didn't think you knew."

Didn't think I knew? Now he was utterly confused. How could he not know? This was about what *he* had done.

Wasn't it?

He took Zoey's arm again and drew her toward the elevator. They were both silent on the trip down. Zoey was like someone in a fever. Her face was flushed. She stared with bright, agitated eyes. Outside in the cooler air she gasped, as if she'd been suffocating.

Jake led her to a bench and sat her down. "I want you to tell me exactly what happened up there, Zoey," he said.

"Why are you here?" Zoey asked.

"I have study hall last period," Jake said. "You know that. And practice is starting late because Coach had something he had to go to."

“You weren’t supposed to know,” Zoey said again.

“That you were coming here?”

Zoey shrugged. “Any of it.” Suddenly she put her hand on his. “I didn’t want your family to be hurt, either.”

Jake took a deep breath. “Look, Zoey, I only know some of it,” he said, lying. He knew none of it. Whatever it was. “I want you to tell me what you said to my dad. Word for word. That way I’ll be prepared, okay?”

Then Zoey told him.

Fourteen

After last period Claire went out to the football bleachers, expecting to do some homework while she watched Jake practice. He could use the show of support and besides, there was a magnificent, towering thunderhead, a cumulo-nimbus formation, to the south. The top was so high it had been sheared flat by the high-altitude winds. She could watch the sky, her greatest fascination, in between pretending to watch Jake.

Lucas went from last period to the football field, expecting to find Zoey. She'd said she was working on her story, and he knew that involved the football team. He also knew, and had known from the start, that Jake was the one who had been using. It was one of several secrets he had been keeping. People had an annoying habit of telling him their secrets—Christopher, Jake, Louise Kronenberger . . .

Claire saw Jake coming from the direction of town. Zoey was with him, walking close by his side. Why? Why were they coming from the direction of town, and why were they together coming from that direction?

* * *

Lucas saw them, too, and he was close enough to see that they were holding hands. Holding hands. Zoey and Jake. Jake, who never seemed to quite completely disappear from her life. It was the Freddy Kreuger of relationships—it never seemed permanently dead. He always had the feeling that beyond that next squeaky door, or just beneath the surface of that swampy pond, bingo! Up would pop Jake. And sure enough, here he was.

Claire noticed the hand holding, too. She had to stare hard to be sure, but yes, just then the two of them had swung their hands together, in unison. Unbelievable. Holding hands. With Zoey. No, no, this was not how things happened. Zoey might have Lucas when Claire was done with him; Nina might even have Benjamin when she was done with him. But she hadn't grown tired of Jake yet. When she did, then . . . whatever. But this was totally out of order.

Lucas saw Claire, far off across the field, over the heads of the bouncing cheerleaders practicing ragged cheers, a distant but easily identifiable figure on the bleachers. Claire was staring at the same sight he was watching—Jake with Zoey in deep, personal conversation. Jake touching Zoey's arm. Zoey nodding. Zoey grabbing his hand and almost shaking it, telling him something very earnestly. Jake nodding yes.

Then Claire saw it. Zoey and Jake in a long . . . long . . . very long hug. Breaking free and Zoey . . .

* * *

Yes, Lucas confirmed to himself. It had been a kiss. A kiss on Jake's cheek. Damn it. Damn him. Damn her.

. . . a definite kiss, Claire noted. Just a cheek, but a kiss just the same. Well. Added to Louise Kronenberger's little jab today, it was enough to make a suspicious person wonder. And she was a suspicious person. Was there a more cunning side to Jake? Was he not quite the simple person he seemed to be? Did he actually believe that she, Claire Geiger, was going to be used? By *him*?

No wonder, Lucas thought coldly. No wonder Zoey had been so distant ever since Vermont. Had something happened between her and Jake even there? He drifted back from the field, not wanting to be seen, melting back into the milling crowd on its way to the parking lot. There was no point in listening to some long string of explanations from Zoey. Or, worse yet, a confirmation of what he suspected.

Claire climbed down from the bleachers and moved swiftly out of sight behind them. She wasn't about to play the role of the poor, jealous girlfriend. So. So maybe Jake wasn't quite the straightforward, always-up-front guy she had imagined. No, maybe not.

She checked her watch. Still time to grab the four o'clock ferry home. Well, well. What exactly had happened? Had Zoey gone after Jake on the drug story and had Jake then turned her around? Perhaps Jake had put on a convincing show, telling Zoey that he still cared about her and how could she expose him to public scorn and so on.

Right. Jake put on a show. That was likely. Jake,

who stammered like an idiot anytime he had to lie. Jake, being nefarious enough to pretend to care for Zoey just so she'd lay off the story? Uh-huh. Yeah, Jake was nefarious, all right. A real master manipulator.

No, the fact was that he *did* still care for Zoey. He always had, Claire told herself. Of course he did. Zoey was just his type. Snow White and the slightly tarnished Prince. They were perfect together.

She realized she was seething, walking down Mainsail Street with a face for murder. She paused in front of a candy store and pretended to look at the display, while in fact she was checking her own reflection. Yes, far too much anger. Far too much emotion. Far, far too upset just because *her* boyfriend had been in a deep, intimate conversation with Zoey "I'm-ever-so-good" Passmore. Just because he had put his arms around her and squeezed her skinny, flat-chested body against his. And held her far too long.

She resumed her walk, laboring to keep her face blank, but still breathing like Darth Vader.

What a rush of emotion, a rational corner of her mind observed. *You're getting unusually upset, Claire. You're acting as if you're jealous, which is impossible.*

It took me by surprise, she argued with herself. *I wasn't prepared. I didn't expect to see it. Jake with Zoey!*

Lucas crossed her path, just in front of her. He was striding along with energetic concentration.

"Lucas," she called out.

He stopped and turned. "What?" he snapped. "Oh. It's you."

"You were back there, weren't you?"

His eyes were fierce. "Back there? You mean *your*

boyfriend copping a cheap feel off *my* girlfriend? Yeah, I was back there.''

''I'm sure you're misinterpreting things.''

''Yeah, they were probably sharing some class notes. Or maybe discussing world peace.''

Claire met his dark, mistrustful glare with one of her own. ''Maybe we're overreacting.''

''She's been cold to me ever since we came back from Vermont,'' Lucas snapped. ''I thought it was over something else. She puts me through hell, makes me think it's me that's the problem, and all the time it's about Jake. She was even talking about him when we were there. Jake this and Jake that. And with all the stuff I know about Jake McRoyan, he ought to be more careful whose girlfriend he's playing grab-ass with.''

Claire thought of pointing out that in no way had Jake been playing grab-ass, but that was of much less importance than Lucas's remark about knowing. ''What do you mean, all the stuff you know about Jake?''

Lucas seemed about to answer, but then just looked sullen.

Claire took a shot in the dark. ''You mean about Jake getting suspended from the team?''

''Yes, I know about that,'' Lucas admitted. ''Unfortunately, people have this habit of telling me stuff, or else I just have bad luck and happen to be in the wrong places at the wrong times. Like about five minutes ago,'' he added bitterly.

''And I guess you know about Jake and Louise?'' Claire said, holding her breath.

''Yeah!'' Lucas said, excited. ''I should just tell Zoey about that. Then see how much she likes Jake. He's not exactly the same old Jake she used to go out with.'' Then, calmer, he shot a glance at Claire. ''I guess that must have pissed you off, too, huh?''

''Yes,'' Claire said, now cold as ice. ''It must have.''

Benjamin shifted the bass on the portable CD player and adjusted his earphones. His favorite part of Bach's B Minor Mass was coming—the ''Dona Nobis Pacem,'' a prayer for peace, as sublime a piece of music as he had ever heard.

He could feel the familiar vibration of the ferry's engines. There was a gentle and not too cold breeze, though once out on the water the temperature dropped a sharp ten degrees. He could tell the bay was choppy because from time to time the breeze would catch the top of a wave and hurl its cold spray against the side of his face. On the back of his neck he could just feel the slanting rays of a failing sun, sliding down behind the buildings of Weymouth. Everywhere was the smell of brine. And like distant echoes, he could hear through the music the calls of gulls following the ferry and hoping for a handout.

He felt a soft impact beside him, and the warmth of a body now touching his right arm. The scent of coconut shampoo and an unlit cigarette.

Nina. She was waiting till he was done with the music, perhaps watching his face, perhaps looking around at what sounded and smelled and felt like a beautiful world.

The music died away and he pulled off his earphones. ''Hi.''

''Hi. What were you listening to?''

''Red Hot Chili Peppers.''

''Liar. It was that Bach guy.''

Benjamin smiled. "Chili Peppers are just Bach with more *f* words. Many more."

He felt warmth on his cheek, the undefinable sense of someone very near, then soft lips on his own.

"What was that for?" he asked, smiling at the flood of warmth that rushed through him. "Not that I'm complaining."

"I just felt like it. Is it okay when I just do that? I mean, does it embarrass you or anything?"

"You know what it does?" he asked. "It makes me think there really are things even better than music."

"Even Bach?" Mock surprise mixed with genuine pleasure.

"Hmm. Certainly better than Red Hot Chili Peppers."

"I have a feeling that no matter which way I take that, it will work out to be an insult," Nina said.

Benjamin let his hand drift right, made contact with her leg, hovered discreetly above till he found her hand. He entwined his fingers through hers and then raised her hand to his lips. "I would never mean any insult."

Nina snuggled closer.

"How come you're not with the girls?" Benjamin asked. "Breaking with tradition?"

"Nah, Aisha and your sister are both in lousy moods. They don't even know I'm not there, probably."

"And *your* sister?"

"Claire missed the boat. Or else—oh, yeah. Wednesday's the day her coven meets."

Benjamin laughed. "Black mass?"

"She's going to conjure up the devil. She has him

on speed-dial now. They're always chatting, exchanging helpful hints, recipes and so on."

Benjamin laughed again. He didn't really resent Claire for dumping him. Not really. But he did get a certain pleasure from Nina's occasional well-placed shots at her sister. After a pause he said, "Zoey has seemed preoccupied lately."

"Tell me about it. Her and Aisha both. Maybe they're having that thing when girls are around each other a lot and their periods start coming at the same time. Maybe it's synchronized PMS."

"An exhibition sport at the Olympics," Benjamin said.

"That was going to be my joke. You can't be stealing my punch lines."

"Or else what?"

"Oh, nothing," Nina said too innocently.

"Don't flip me off, Nina," he warned.

"Damn."

"So they're okay, though, right? Zoey and Aisha?"

A deep breath. "Zoey's your sister," Nina said, sounding a little cranky. "The deal is supposed to be that she doesn't spy on you for me, or me for you, and that we don't spy on her for each other. Otherwise, total chaos. The end of civilization as we know it. Besides, I don't know what her problem is. She made up with Lucas and all."

"Cool. Can you come over this evening to read to me?" he asked.

"Sure. Read what?"

He shrugged. "I don't know. Whatever I can come up with as a good excuse to have you with me."

"Okay." A lingering shyness in her voice.

Benjamin had to remind himself that for all her seeming boldness, underneath it Nina was still somewhat uncertain and even frightened in her romantic life. It made him want all the more to protect her.

He put his arm around her shoulders and held her close. There was something he wanted to tell her at that moment. A feeling that had been growing in him, becoming more certain, more powerful. He held back, though her nearness, the feel of her resting against him, the heartbreaking sweetness he couldn't fail to recognize just below the prickly surface, all conspired to make silence almost impossible. So he said the silent words in his mind. *I love you, Nina. I love you.*

"What?" she asked, sounding almost drowsy.

He kissed the top of her head. "I didn't say anything."

Zoey was aware that Nina had moved away to be with Benjamin. That was good. It was good that they were doing so well. Good for Nina that she had Benjamin, and good for Benjamin also. Her two favorite people in the world. Along with her father.

She was also aware that Aisha was in some kind of a funk, staring off toward the approaching island, not talking, not doing her homework or reading. And normally Zoey would have investigated, but at the moment her mind was filled with her own problems.

The scene between Mr. McRoyan and her had left Zoey feeling dirty somehow. And what had followed with Jake was even worse in some ways. She realized now that Jake had no idea what was going on between his father and her mother. Zoey had been the one to deliver that news to him, which wasn't what she had intended.

She had done nothing but make mistakes right from

the start. She shouldn't have let her mother see how angry she was. She should have remembered that Jake sometimes stopped by his father's office. She probably should have just closed her eyes to the whole thing.

It was all part of what she now saw as her own naiveté. It was true—she wasn't ready to grow up. That was the reason for her fight with Lucas. And it was the reason she was behaving irrationally over this now. After all, half the kids at school came from broken homes. And it wasn't like she was a little kid who couldn't understand what was going on. She was seventeen, a high school senior. Soon she would be at college, making her own life away from her parents. What did it really matter if her mother and father broke up?

Except that it did matter. She didn't care if divorces and broken homes were commonplace. This was *her* family. Hers and Benjamin's. What would happen if there was a divorce? Would her mother or father have to move away? And who would Zoey end up living with? And where?

But the most terrible image, the one that kept appearing and reappearing in her mind's eye, was the image of her father when he found out the truth. That image seared her thoughts so painfully that she had to look away.

Zoey hugged herself, feeling lonely and overwhelmed. Why wasn't Lucas here? It would have felt good to be in Lucas's arms now, as Nina was in Benjamin's. Only Lucas wasn't on the ferry. Neither, for that matter, was Claire.

Claire was probably at the practice, cheering Jake on. He would need all the support he could get. But where was Lucas?

If Lucas were here, he would make her feel better. And he would drive from her mind the disturbing memory of the way she had felt when Jake had taken her in his arms.

Fifteen

Claire stepped on the gas and her father's big Mercedes accelerated into a turn. She down-shifted and powered through, with trees flashing by on one side and a long drop to the surf-battered rocks below. She had to fight the centrifugal force that nearly tore her away from the wheel. A glance confirmed that Lucas was clutching the dashboard in a way that might well leave permanent marks.

"I'm not scaring you, am I?" she asked nonchalantly.

"Nah. What's scary about plunging two hundred feet straight down the side of a cliff so that we end up being a meal for crabs?"

They were driving around because neither of them could think of anything else to do. They were driving around because the alternative was getting on the ferry with Zoey and going back to the island. They were driving around together because the mere act of being together was a slap at Jake and Zoey respectively and it made them both feel liberated.

Claire took the next curve slower. "I suppose you're thinking about the last time you went driving with me."

Lucas gave her a cautious look. "Possible."

Their last drive had been two years earlier. Lucas, Jake's big brother Wade, and her. All three drunk. Claire driving. Into a tree, killing Wade, leaving her without memory of the event and causing Lucas's wrongful imprisonment.

Claire slowed down more. It wasn't as if Lucas had no reason to worry. By the next curve she was barely above the speed limit, and even had time to look at the scenery. This section of road wound along classically rugged mainland coast. Through the trees they glimpsed gray swells and explosions of white foam, the slow-motion destruction of the land by the sea as it chewed the cliffs into boulders and rock, and eventually, a million years in the future, into sand.

A brief glance toward the south showed the ferry, a tiny yellow, black, and white toy, crossing sparkling water.

"Let's keep driving till we're back in Vermont," Lucas said after a long silence.

"That's the other direction."

"That's where everything started to go to hell," Lucas said.

"I had thought the trip was pretty much a success," Claire said. "Jake and I were together and everything was fine."

"Zoey and I weren't fine."

"I guess Jake and I weren't, either, given what we just saw."

"You know, you two guys were sort of broken up when he . . . you know, when he and Louise . . ." Lucas said, declining into a mumble.

"At a loss for words?" Claire asked dryly.

"Plus, he was hammered," Lucas offered.

"Uh-huh."

Another long silence, broken again by Lucas. "And

you know Louise. She even came on to me, at the homecoming dance. I'm sure it didn't mean anything to her, and we both know it didn't mean anything to Jake."

"So did you take up her offer?" Claire asked lightly.

"No," Lucas said, laughing a little. "But I wasn't drunk and I hadn't just gotten suspended from the football team and I wasn't all messed up over a girl who—" He prudently let the rest of the thought go unspoken.

"A girl who was responsible for the death of Jake's brother," Claire concluded for him.

"Ancient history," Lucas said.

"Jake and Zoey were supposed to be ancient history, too," Claire reminded him. "History doesn't always stay buried. Old relationships never seem to completely die."

"Like you and Benjamin?"

Claire smiled her wintry smile. "He wasn't my *first* boyfriend." She waited for Lucas's response. It was slow in coming.

"Speaking of ancient history," he said softly, looking out the window.

Claire braked behind a slow-moving pickup truck. She craned her neck to look around it and see some of the road ahead. There were at least a couple of hundred yards of road clear of oncoming traffic. "Hold on," she said. She stepped on the gas and swung into the oncoming lane, accelerating past the truck and ducking to safety just a few feet from an onrushing car whose driver leaned on his horn and shook his fist.

"You have air bags in this thing?" Lucas asked.

Again, a long silence. Claire knew she should let it

alone. She had made her little foray, bringing up old times, and Lucas had let it drop. And there was no good purpose to be served by bringing it up again.

Except that she was still coldly furious with Jake. Sleeping with Louise. The long open display of affection with Zoey. Unacceptable. She had gone through a lot to make Jake hers. And she didn't at all like the idea that after everything she'd done, he still had his thoughts on other girls.

She would have thought that of all the guys she knew, Jake would have been the one who was, well, easiest to control. It sounded harsh, but there it was. She had manipulated Jake, wringing from him his acceptance and forgiveness and, she had imagined, his devotion. And all the time he'd been savoring memories of Louise, and no doubt keeping in a secret part of his heart some lingering hope that he might get back together with Zoey.

"You were my first serious kiss," Claire said.

Lucas started as if he'd been caught in a guilty thought. Then he put on a careless tone and a no-big-deal smile. "You were my first, serious or not."

"You weren't bad for a first time," Claire said. It was pretty tacky, flirting this openly with Lucas. But then, he had agreed to go for a drive with her. And he was as pissed at Zoey as Claire was with Jake. "Do you remember it?"

Lucas shifted on the leather seat. "We were swimming, right?"

He remembered. That was obvious from the guilty look on his face and the way he kept changing positions.

"Yes, we were swimming down at Town Beach. You were very cute. You asked me in this squeaky voice if you could kiss me. And I said yes."

Lucas nodded.

"I remember you were surprised when I put my tongue in your mouth." She rolled her eyes. "And that suit I was wearing. The top was like two sizes too small because I'd bought it the year before, and I was practically—"

"Um, Claire?" Lucas crossed his legs.

"Yes?"

"Why are you doing this?"

"Doing what?"

"Trying to make me get—" He sucked in a deep breath. "Trying to make me . . . You know."

Claire laughed. "I guess I'm pissed off at Jake."

"So you thought you'd make yourself feel better by seeing if you could get me all worked up?"

"Sounds so sleazy when you put it that way," Claire said. "Did it work?"

"Almost as well as it did back then," Lucas admitted. "God. I'll tell you, Claire. After that day on the beach I would have fought a swamp full of alligators armed with a Popsicle stick for you."

"I'll remember that if I ever have an alligator problem."

Lucas shook his head. "You know, you're a strange and not exactly nice girl, Claire."

"I know."

"It will never work with you and Jake, you realize. Not for long, anyway."

"You could be right," Claire allowed. But then, "long" was a relative term. "Shall we head back?"

"Sure. I don't think driving around any more is going to make our problems go away."

Claire swung the car off onto the shoulder of the road, then pulled it into a U-turn.

"Just out of curiosity," Lucas asked, "how far

were you prepared to go with me to get back at Jake?''

Claire smiled. ''Maybe we'll find out someday. If you're right about Jake and me. And if I'm right about you and Zoey.''

By the time the ferry had landed, Aisha had a plan. But she had to wait two long hours, during which time she paced back and forth in her room, sometimes listening to music, other times in silence so she could concentrate.

There was no doubt in her mind what Christopher had been doing at lunch today. He had bought a gun. As simple as that—he had bought a gun.

And there wasn't very much doubt as to what he intended to use it for. At the very least he would carry it around and wait for the skin-heads to take a second shot at him. But what were the odds of that happening? The far more terrifying possibility was that Christopher actually planned to find the guys who had beaten him up and retaliate.

Just the thought of it made her want to throw up. Not through any pity for the creeps, but because it would be the end of Christopher as the boy, and even man, that he had been.

At first she'd worried that he might be planning to do it tonight. But then she'd realized that Christopher was due to cook at Passmores' tonight. It almost made her laugh. Christopher might be thinking of taking human life, but he would never think of just dumping work.

It was insane. But then, it was an insane situation. One she was not going to allow to get any worse.

She went through the motions of dinner with her family, of doing the dishes, of pretending to start on her homework. Then, at eight o'clock, she gathered up the parcel she had prepared and went outside into the night. She rode her bike, coasting down the long slope of Climbing Way, cutting left to pedal past Town Beach, panting as much from excitement as exertion.

The lights of Weymouth sparkled and wavered across the black sea. Other lights—Jake's house, the few other still-occupied houses interspersed between the boarded-up summer rentals and small hotels—spilled faint illumination onto the sand-strewn road. As usual, there was no traffic on the road, unless you counted the ancient Irish setter who gave her a thoughtful look as she passed.

She pulled up in front of Christopher's rooming house and leaned the bike against the front porch railing. If she was lucky, no one would see her or say anything. But if the landlady was around, Aisha had a plan. She'd show her the parcel and tell her it was a gift for Christopher that she just wanted to drop off in his room.

She went inside and up the creaky, slightly creepy staircase to Christopher's door unchallenged. Tired sixties rock escaped from one of the rooms down the dark hall.

Christopher's door was locked, but she found the key she'd seen him hide beneath an edge of the stair carpeting. She opened the door.

"Christopher?" she asked the emptiness.

Silence. She closed the door behind her and snapped on the light. The room was octagonal, within a tower that formed the corner of the Victorian structure. He had a bed, neatly made. A small kitchenette in one corner, all the mismatched dishes cleaned and drying in the rack. A small black-and-white TV sitting on a chair with a wire hanger twisted into an antenna.

"So where would you hide it, Christopher?" she whispered. Talking to herself dispelled some of the strangeness of being here without him.

She crossed to his bed and lifted the thin mattress. A *Playboy* magazine. No gun.

For a moment she considered the idea of taking the magazine and throwing it away. That would give him something to think about. But no, she was only after the gun. Dirty magazines didn't kill people or ruin lives.

She opened the dresser drawers, one by one. Top drawer was socks and underwear. Plain white cotton briefs. She was almost disappointed. Somehow she'd suspected Christopher might have gone for something more showy. In a way, it was reassuring. A guy who wore plain white cotton briefs couldn't be too crazy, could he? Certainly not crazy enough to use a gun.

"No, just crazy enough to buy one from some white trash dirtbag on the street. Perfectly sane. Nothing to worry about, Aisha."

Second drawer, T-shirts, two sweaters, gloves.

Third drawer, mostly empty but for a pair of shorts. And the last drawer held miscellaneous junk like paper, a few loose tapes, a pad of paper, scattered pencils and pens.

No gun.

Half an hour later she was as certain as she could be. The gun wasn't here. Could she have been wrong? Could it be that despite what she'd thought she'd seen, he didn't really buy a gun? Or . . .

A pathetic hope, probably, but he could have grown a brain at the last minute and decided to get rid of it.

Aisha lay back on his bed and stared up at his ceiling. The paint was peeling back from a water stain.

Why did she care? It wasn't like she was in love with him, at least not anymore. Not since she'd realized what a snake he was. Only she did still care enough that she couldn't stand by and let him destroy himself. She did still care that much.

She felt defeated. She'd thought she was being so clever. She would find the gun, take it, and throw it off the point into the fast-moving current.

Only she hadn't found the gun. And now she would have to make the probably doomed attempt to talk him out of it.

Aisha got up, turned off the light, and lay back down again. When he came home, she would talk him out of it. She would do whatever it took to save him from himself.

Although she no longer loved him.

Sixteen

Christopher read the ticket the waitress had slapped on the stainless steel counter. He moved to pull a broiler plate of fish from the reach-in, took off the plastic wrap, and slid it into the oven. He squatted, pulled the pan of steaks from the second reach-in, selected a nicely marbled strip, stood up, and tossed it on the grill.

Then he went to the walk-in, closed the door behind him, and pulled the gun from his pocket. It wasn't a big gun, or especially beautiful. Just dull blue steel, worn on the end of the barrel, a blunt little automatic. He pressed the button that ejected the clip and looked at the top bullet. A stubby brass casing topped by a dull lead slug, no bigger than the fingernail on his little finger. Thirty-eight caliber. Hollow point, so that the slug would flatten out on impact.

He had wanted a nine millimeter. Nines were the gun of choice in Sandtown, the Baltimore neighborhood where he had grown up. Everyone who was anyone had a nine. But no nine millimeters had been available, and a thirty-eight would do the job.

He put the gun back in his pocket. It was heavy and tugged at that side of his pants.

He checked his fish, turned the steak, made sure no

other tickets were waiting, and went back to the walk-in. He took out the gun and struck a pose, pointing it at a box of lettuce.

"Bang," he said.

He whirled and aimed it square at a half-empty number ten jar of Thousand Island dressing. "Pow. Pow."

If only he'd had this when the skinheads had jumped him. He'd have liked to see the looks on their faces. "Going to kick my ass?" he said in a tough voice. "You'd better talk to my friend about that." He whipped the gun up from his side, leveling it at his remembered foes. At the guy he had seen through the window.

"Not so tough now, huh?"

He put the gun back in his pocket and went out to plate up the food. "Pick up!" he yelled.

He was impatient for the waitress to pick up the order. He wanted to check just one more thing on the gun. He wanted to be sure he knew exactly how to click off the safety.

The waitress came. Christopher ducked back inside the walk-in and took out the gun. Yes, he could do it with his thumb. It was awkward, but he could snap off the safety with his thumb. He did it several times. The feel of the gun became even more powerful when the safety was off. Now just the slightest pressure on the trigger . . .

He put the gun back in his pocket, suddenly feeling scared. What if it went off? What if he accidentally shot someone?

But had he put the safety back on? He took it out again and checked. God, the safety had been off! He clicked it on and put the gun away again.

Over the next few hours he took it out many more

times. Too many to remember or count. He rushed through the final cleanup of the kitchen at the end of the night and did the minimal amount of prep work.

He went out front to check with Ms. Passmore and see if it was okay to leave. But the waitress was covering the bar. Ms. Passmore had stepped outside.

Christopher found her around the corner. She was deep in conversation with a man. Christopher was fairly sure it was Mr. McRoyan, Jake's father. Their low voices sounded tense and upset. He thought of backing away, but Ms. Passmore had spotted him.

"What is it, Christopher?"

"I just wanted to check with you before I took off."

"Go ahead. See you tomorrow."

On the way home from work, he pulled his bike to a stop to check the gun again.

He went up the stairs to his apartment. He had to take the gun out of his pocket again to reach his keys. He unlocked his door.

But what if someone had broken in? There wasn't any crime to speak of on Chatham Island, but what if? Maybe the skinheads had tracked him down, found out where he lived, and broken in. Maybe they were waiting for him right now.

Well, they'd get a surprise, wouldn't they?

He pulled out the gun, holding it in a sweaty hand. He opened the door.

There *was* someone inside!

Zoey recognized the knock on the front door. She put down the knife and the peanut butter, wiping her hands on a paper towel, and went to open the door. From the family room came the sound of the TV. From Benjamin's room came the sound of music,

Pearl Jam, which meant that Nina was still in there, though it was getting late.

Lucas stood under the porch light, looking truculent.

"Hi, come on in," Zoey said, trying to plaster on a big smile.

Lucas seemed hesitant, as if he wanted to kiss her but wasn't sure. Zoey solved the problem for him by leaning forward and giving him a quick kiss on the side of his mouth.

He smiled. "Peanut butter?"

"Oh, sorry." She wiped her mouth with the back of her hand.

"It's okay. I like peanut butter."

He followed her inside. She retrieved her sandwich and then led him toward the family room. He held her back.

"I thought we could go up to your room."

"Well, I was kind of keeping my dad company," she said.

"We hung with your dad last night," Lucas said plaintively.

Zoey flushed. Of course Lucas didn't understand why she wanted to be with her dad, she realized. He wanted to go upstairs and make out. But this wasn't the day for making out.

She slid a consoling hand into the pocket where he'd stuck his own hand. "Just a little while, okay?"

"I think we need to talk about something," he said doggedly.

Zoey almost laughed. Lucas wanted to *talk*? Not likely. "Sure you do," she said teasingly.

"I saw you and Jake at the football field today," he said.

"That was nothing," Zoey said quickly. Too quickly; it sounded suspicious.

"He was feeling you up in front of the whole school."

"He was not," Zoey said, outraged.

"You want to do this here, where your dad or Benjamin might walk out and hear everything we're saying?"

Zoey gritted her teeth. Just what she needed now. More grief from Lucas. She marched up the stairs, threw open the door, and sat stiffly on the edge of her bed, arms crossed, still, unfortunately, holding her sandwich.

Lucas closed the door behind him. He also crossed his arms and looked at her expectantly. "Okay, I'm listening."

"For what?"

"To hear why you were letting Jake grope you, that's what for."

"He was not *groping* me. Not everyone has your sex-obsessed mind, Lucas. Not everyone thinks a friendly hug is an excuse to start groping."

"Oh. So now he's better than me, right?"

"Maybe he's just not stuck on one topic all the time. Did it ever occur to you that what you saw may have had nothing to do with me and Jake?"

He laughed derisively. "Yeah, I figured when he was groping you it probably had to do with finding a cure for cancer."

"Sometimes you really make me mad, Lucas," Zoey said bitterly. Couldn't he get it through his head that this wasn't what he thought? She had hugged Jake because he was hurting after finding out about his father. And he had hugged her back because he cared about her and how she felt.

Lucas narrowed his eyes. "Did you get anywhere on that drug story?"

Zoey was taken aback. What was this about now? "What does that have to do with anything?"

"It was Jake, you know. Jake got drunk before the homecoming game and used some coke to get fired up for the game. I told you that night, only of course you didn't want to believe anything bad about Jake the Saint. And then you pretend you're going to do this story, only see, it would have to be about Jake."

"I know it's Jake," Zoey said flatly. "I found out this morning. Claire told me."

Lucas looked disappointed, but he redoubled his attack. "There's something else that even Claire didn't know about until this afternoon."

Zoey tried to look utterly indifferent, but Lucas plowed on.

"See, even Claire didn't know where Jake ended up that night after the game."

"You're going to tell me anyway, so go ahead."

"He ended up with Louise Kronenberger. *With* Louise. Very *with* Louise. Saint Jake, coked, hammered, and showing his muscles to Lay-Down Louise." He laughed cruelly. "Yeah, he's a much nicer person than me, Zoey."

Zoey covered her mouth with her hand. She felt like she'd been slapped. One more blow. Just one more rude surprise. Lucas, in a van in Vermont telling her he wouldn't wait forever . . . the monstrous sight of her mother . . . and now Jake. . . . It was like some busy demon was running around smashing everything she believed.

"Just leave, Lucas," she whispered.

"Wow, I'm sorry to tell you the truth about good

old Jake. I'm sorry if I screwed up your plan to get back together with him."

Suddenly, surprising herself even more than Lucas, Zoey slammed her two fists violently down on the edge of the bed. "Everybody just leave me alone! Just leave me alone!"

"You're messed up, Zoey," Lucas said.

Zoey sagged, the violence burned out as quickly as it had kindled. "Yes. I am messed up," she said softly. "I am messed up beyond belief." Through sudden tears she saw Lucas's eyes soften. He took a step toward her. She put up her hand. "Don't. You can't help me."

"I—I could try," he said quietly.

"You've done a great job so far," Zoey said bitterly. "The person I should be able to turn to really only cares about whether he can get me to have sex with him. It's all anyone cares about, isn't it? You think people are your family and you can trust them, but that's all it is. Themselves. Just whatever they want for themselves. Forget everyone else and what they want, right? Someone else gets hurt, too bad. And they're doing all these things and don't even care. Oh, sorry, Zoey. Sorry if I destroyed your family and now you have to be thinking all the time 'what's next?' "

"Zoey, what are you talking about?"

"About . . . everything. Never mind. It's none of your business because all you want is to sleep with me, right, Lucas?"

"I love you, Zoey," he said in a quiet voice.

"Then it's settled. Come on, let's do it. Everyone else is, right? Why not?" She began tugging at the buttons of her blouse. "Come on, Lucas. You can do whatever you want and then you can go home and forget it, right?"

"Zoey, what is happening with you?" Quiet, worried.

"I'm growing up," she sneered, too full of fury to care that he was reaching out to her. "Isn't that what I'm supposed to do? Aren't I supposed to grow up and realize what people are really like?"

"Zoey, look—"

"No. Just get out, Lucas."

"I want to help."

Zoey sank back on her bed, utterly exhausted. "Just go away. Everyone just go away."

To my daughter,
On your fourteenth birthday. Well, you're definitely a teenager now. The day before yesterday we had a big fight because I told you I didn't think you should go to the movies alone with Jake. You told me I was hopelessly old, that I didn't understand that it was perfectly normal to be going on dates at almost fourteen. Wow. I want you to know that "hopelessly old" crack hit home. Probably because it's what I

used to tell my mother.

I just didn't want you to start getting all involved with guys at your age. What you don't know yet (but will someday) is that they aren't just like girlfriends. Men can break your heart, and you can break theirs. Not that Jake is exactly a man Remember last month when we found him stuffed in one of our trash cans and his big brother had tied down the lid?

Still, you haven't turned rotten or anything, despite being a teenager.

You're still basically pretty sweet. Especially around Benjamin. He's been going through a bad time, realizing that he's fallen behind because of the surgeries and rehab and all, and now he's in the same grade as his little sister. But you've handled it with such style it really makes your dad and me proud. Sometimes we wonder how the two of us managed to produce such great kids.

You didn't want the usual party this year, so we dropped you and your friends off for pizza, movies, and video games. Then you realized, too late to do anything about it, that it would mean leaving Benjamin out. You were so devastated. You haven't learned yet that there are times when no matter how hard you try not to, you hurt people anyway. You're not very tough or cynical, Zoey. Maybe this will mean you'll always be easily hurt by others. But it will also mean you'll never be cruel, so it's a good thing.

Two more years and I'll give you this

book. You've changed so much
in just the last year I
wonder what you will be
then?

Seventeen

Aisha woke disoriented. Not her bed. Where was she?

A loud, questioning voice, tense, even threatening. A shape silhouetted in an open doorway.

Christopher.

"I said who's in there?"

"It's me," Aisha said. "It's me, Aisha."

The shape seemed to shrink to mere human proportions. He gave a relieved laugh. "Damn, you scared the hell out of me."

"Sorry. I fell asleep waiting for you." Aisha sat up.

Christopher didn't turn on the light. He came to her, sat down beside her, very close. "This is a very nice surprise."

Aisha accepted his kiss and returned it. His arms held her close. Her hand came to rest against something hard and cold. Recognition was immediate.

"What's that?" she asked.

"Nothing," he lied.

Aisha pushed him away. "It's not nothing."

"My keys."

"It's a gun, Christopher."

Silence.

She pushed him farther away and stood up. She

searched for the lamp and found the switch. They both blinked in the sudden illumination.

"I saw you buy it," Aisha admitted.

Christopher looked alarmed. "Did anyone else see me, do you think?"

"I don't think so, no. You can still get rid of it and no one will ever know."

"Get rid of it?" He laughed incredulously. "Why would I want to get rid of it?"

"You have to get rid of it, Christopher. That's why I came here tonight. I was going to take it from you."

He stood up. His eyes were narrowed and suspicious. His right hand strayed unconsciously to the gun, a sharp-edged lump in his pocket. "I went to a lot of trouble to buy it, Eesh."

"Christopher, you can't do this."

"Can't do what?"

"Oh, don't treat me like I'm an idiot, Christopher!" Aisha shouted. "Don't you think I know what you're planning?"

"I'm not planning anything. I'm just planning that the next time someone tries to jump me, I can protect myself." He smiled, softening his confrontational tone. "It's no big thing, Aisha. Back in Baltimore, back in Sandtown, everyone had a gun."

"Yeah, and it was a real paradise, wasn't it?"

His eyes clouded. His jaw was stubborn. "Look, I can't let it stand the way it is, Eesh." He shook his head as if he were helpless in the matter. As if he was really terribly sorry, but he had no choice. "I can't let it stand."

"Christopher, you can't do this," she pleaded.

"You don't understand," he said heavily. "I'm a man. A man doesn't let himself be hurt without hurting back. A man doesn't let himself be kicked and pounded on without making someone pay."

"Christopher, I thought . . . I mean, all the time you were at my house, all the time we were in Vermont, you seemed normal. You seemed like you were dealing with—"

"I *was* dealing with it," he blazed, rounding on her. He thrust a finger in her face, spitting the words. "I was dealing with it because I knew the day would come when I would make them pay. Perfectly calm, absolutely no problem, as long as I knew that the day would come. I waited. I can be patient when I have to be. I waited and said okay, Christopher, it's bad, but you hang in there and you'll get yours back. Now the time has come."

"Christopher—" she began, but he was past listening now.

"They kicked me, Aisha. I was on the ground and they kicked me and called me a nigger and—" He clasped his hands together, struggling to control the rage. Then, in a softer, yet more dangerous voice, "They spit on me, Eesh. People don't spit on me. No." He shook his head. "No, that doesn't happen. No one spits on me and calls me a nigger and just walks away thinking, hey, that was cool, let's go have a beer."

For a moment Aisha was caught up in his words, in a cold, hard anger. Yes, yes, make the bastards pay. She remembered her first sight of him in the hospital bed. At that moment, given the chance, wouldn't she have struck back as hard as she could? And, after all, would the world mourn the loss of another violent, hate-twisted monster? If the police couldn't do it, didn't Christopher have a right to exact his own revenge? Did they just have to take it and take it and never fight back?

But against all that was the single image that had formed in Aisha's mind and wouldn't go away. The image of Christopher with a gun in his hand, taking a life.

If he did that, if he killed, he would destroy himself as well. That action would take over his life, his personality. He would change to deal with what he had done. He would become hard and cold, just like the gun—lifeless, mechanical. Dead.

"It will be okay," Christopher said. "I'll be careful."

"No, it won't be okay, Christopher," Aisha said, feeling sick with the futility of arguing. Sick with dread. "It will be murder."

"It will be *justice*."

"You will be a person who has deliberately, cold-bloodedly taken a human life," Aisha said. "You won't be the same person ever again. You will never be able to undo or take back that action."

"Look, I'm not going to get caught," he said heatedly.

"Not by the police, maybe. But *you* will know what you've done. And I'll know. And God will know." All a waste of breath. He heard nothing. He understood nothing.

"God?" He laughed derisively. "So you're worried I'll go to hell?"

"*Go* to hell? No, Christopher, you don't understand. If you do this, if you kill, from the moment you pull the trigger you will *be* in hell."

Zoey pulled her Boston Bruins jersey on over her head and a pair of clean white socks on her feet. Her feet sometimes got cold at night. She slipped between crisp sheets and piled her two pillows behind her back. The only light in the room was from the small lamp by her bedside. The clock showed a little after eleven. She should be falling asleep now. She liked to get at least seven hours of sleep, and eight was better. Lately she'd been walking around in a blurry, half-alert state. She felt she hadn't truly slept since Vermont, a million years ago. And yet now, though her legs ached with weariness and her eyes were swollen and sandpapered, she was awake, staring blankly across the room.

It had been an unbelievably long day. It had started with resolve and determination to get control of her life. It had led to terrible scenes with Mr. McRoyan and Jake and ended with a jittery, nerve-wracked explosion between her and Lucas. It was emotional overload. Simply too much to fit into one day, one mind. And now she knew that if she turned off the light and closed her eyes it would all replay, over and over again in her brain, keeping her awake, overwhelming her with its complexity.

Too much. Lucas. Jake. Mr. McRoyan. Her mother and father. Too much.

She would wait until she was utterly exhausted, till she was woozy and passing out, unable to keep her eyelids up another second. Then, if she turned out the light, she might hope for a real sleep. A healing sleep of escape.

Normally she would write in her journal now. Only her journal was long since gone. Part of the landfill.

Or she might read. Except that as she scanned the shelves of her bookshelf, all she saw was one type of romance or another. Escapism. Yes, she wanted to escape, but now all of that had become part of a grubby reality.

"No," she said wryly. "Romance is not what I

need right now.'' She should have books about . . . well, anything but True Love. True Love wasn't doing too well around the Passmore household lately. Except for Benjamin and Nina, but the way things were going, who knew how long that would last?

She got out of bed and pulled her two favorite quote books from the shelf, then retreated to the heavy warmth of her quilt again.

You can close your eyes to reality but not to memories.

Not the best quote for her attention to focus on first, since it was precisely memory that she wanted to avoid.

Downstairs, she heard her mother come home. The door closing.

Neither man nor woman can be worth anything until they have discovered that they are fools.

The squeak of the third step. The sudden intrusion of memory. Of *him* hurrying away on that day. The image still made her skin crawl. How she had hated him. But earlier today, sitting disgusted and ashamed in his office, she hadn't felt the same surge of pure hatred.

The pure and simple truth is rarely pure and never simple.

She heard the door to her parents' room open, then close softly. A hallway separated Zoey's room from theirs. She was trying to do just what the first quote had told her was impossible. She was trying not to remember what she had seen through that bedroom door. Trying not to remember Lucas's angry face in Vermont. Or his angry contempt tonight. Trying not to remember Mr. McRoyan and the way he collapsed on seeing his son. Trying—

A loud murmur of voices from the direction of her parents' room. Anger.

She switched off the light. She didn't know why; it just seemed like the thing to do. Like she could hide if—

A loud shout. Her father's voice. An eruption of more anger than she had ever heard.

Her mother's voice, scaling up, higher, higher, outraged, furious.

Zoey sat in the dark and covered her ears, but now the fight was raging unrestrained. Individual words could be heard, screamed at full volume. *Bastard. Whore. Son of a bitch.*

Others, still worse. Words that never should have come from the mouths of these two people whom she loved.

Zoey clamped a pillow over her head. She felt sick. She felt a deep, churning nausea. Her hands were trembling. Her skin felt crawly.

This had never happened before. She'd had friends who talked nonchalantly about the fights their parents had, but *her* parents had never done this before. Not like this. Not with rage so strong it seemed to vibrate the walls. Not with fury, like some unpredicted hurricane.

Her legs were drawn up to her chest in a fetal position. The knuckles of her hand, clenched white, were in her mouth. She shook. She quivered like a person with a fever. She wanted to throw up, but she couldn't move, and still violent words tore through walls and pillows and all her pitiful defenses to rip at her heart.

It was happening.

It was happening right now, without warning. Like the shattering of an atom, releasing the forces of fire and wind and poison, her family was being shattered.

She could do nothing to stop it. She might have even helped bring it about.

Hatred, loose here in her own family.

A slammed door, rattling the windows. And then a shriek, right at her own door. Her mother's voice, like no voice Zoey had ever heard before.

"Are you happy now, Zoey?" Her mother pounded her fist on the door to Zoey's room, rattling it in the frame. "Are you happy in there, God damn you? Are you happy with what you've done?"

Eighteen

It was after midnight when Zoey lifted her head from her tear-soaked pillow. The house was silent as she crawled from her bed. The sound of her mother's sobbing, coming through the connecting wall to the spare bedroom, had at last subsided.

She had to get out of the house. She had to breathe new, unfouled air. She had to escape from the horrible oppression, the palpable residue of explosive anger.

She pulled on jeans, tucking in her Bruins jersey, then a sweater, a coat. She would be cold, she knew that, because she felt as if her body was already half-dead, unable to generate warmth, all its resources long since exhausted.

She went gently down the stairs, preserving the quiet, temporary peace, afraid lest someone would wake and start the war again. For now there was silence, but for the wind scraping tree branches against the side of the house.

She reached the bottom of the stairs, and, as she had almost expected, Benjamin's door opened.

"Zoey?" he whispered.

Zoey went to him and put her arms around him. He hugged her close, and if every tear had not already been drained, she would have cried again. Instead her chest heaved with dry sobs.

After a long while she pulled away. "I have to get out of here for a while," she said.

"Yeah. Let me get my coat." Then he hesitated. "Is it okay if I go with you?"

She squeezed his hand. "Of course it's okay."

Outside there was air, fresh and cold. They stood in the front yard, midnight-blue figures trimmed with moonlight silver. Their breath rose as steam. They held hands like they had when they were little and Benjamin had been the one to guide his baby sister across the street.

Wordless, they walked out of the yard and down the street over cobblestones slippery with dew, past the gaping black windows of silent, sleeping homes.

They reached the sound of surf, just whispering on the sheltered sand of Town Beach. Doleful buoy bells tolled. Fishing boats at anchor creaked and amplified the slap of the swell against their sides.

They walked out onto the long concrete breakwater that separated the peaceful water of the harbor from the agitated surge of the open sea. Spray erupted to their left, falling over them as a salty rain, freezing and clean. Zoey breathed deeply, drawing each breath to its fullest.

"It was a good idea to come out here," Benjamin said. "The sound of the waves—"

"Yeah."

"Do you . . . Do you hear them like I do, I wonder?" Benjamin asked. "I mean, I hear the sea every day, but still sometimes it's like I've never heard it before. I know you can see it, too, but when you can hear it—*only* hear it—you can feel, or sense, or just

know that it is so vast. So big beyond anything—''
He fell silent.

Zoey sighed, a shuddering sound.

''Did you know about this?'' Benjamin asked. ''About them?''

''Yes.''

Benjamin nodded. ''I thought something was bothering you. I've been kind of thinking about other things, I guess. Nina, mostly.''

''I found out when I came back early from Vermont,'' Zoey said. ''I saw something I wasn't supposed to see.''

Benjamin waited. He was good at waiting.

''I saw Mom and Mr. McRoyan.''

''God, Zoey.'' He sighed. ''That must have been bad.''

''It made me *sick*.'' An almost violent response, surprising her. She wouldn't have thought she had that much emotional energy left in her.

A strong surge exploded over the far end of the breakwater, Christmas-colored rain drifting down before the green and red warning lights.

''I did something kind of creepy,'' Zoey confessed. ''I went up in the attic and found Mom's old letters. I found some from Mr. McRoyan from a long time ago. Supposedly he was in love with Mom while Dad was off in Europe.''

Benjamin pursed his lips thoughtfully. ''I heard something about Europe in all the screaming. It was all kind of confused. Europe and Fred and I think the name Sandra. But I'm probably wrong about that last part.''

They started away from the breakwater, walking hand in hand along Leeward Drive. At this hour the only lights from Weymouth were the pale, almost orange streetlights. All of Chatham Island was dark.

As they walked, Zoey told Benjamin everything she knew. Everything she had done. Benjamin listened without comment until she was done and they turned to follow the road along Big Bite Pond.

"So Mom might have even ended up marrying Mr. McRoyan," Benjamin concluded. "Except that she was pregnant with me. I can't believe they've been together all this time without really loving each other."

"Maybe they have really loved each other," Zoey said. "Maybe it's just complicated."

"Yeah, it's complicated," Benjamin said with a faint whiff of his usual dry humor.

"What do you think will happen now?" Zoey asked.

Benjamin took a while to consider. "It's a pretty straightforward choice—they decide to stay together despite everything, or else they get a divorce."

"What if they get a divorce?"

He shrugged. "I don't know. There's the restaurant. The house. Us." He shrugged again. "I don't know."

"Who would you want to stay with?" Zoey asked.

"I'll stay with the island," he said as if he'd thought it through. "Maybe it's gutless, but last year of high school—I mean, I know the island. I know the school. I don't want to have to go somewhere new, somewhere where I don't know where I am. When I go off to college, that's one thing. I know I'll have to go through the whole process again, learning the streets, counting steps, learning what's safe, and so on. And on and on. But I don't want to have to scope a campus and a new home and throw in half a year of a new school. I have to be kind of selfish. I stick with the island."

"I can't believe we're even having this conversation," Zoey said grimly. "But I'm glad I have you."

"One way or the other, Zo, we have to stay close. We can't let this ever get between us."

"You and me, Benjamin," Zoey said. Tears had edged her eyes again.

"No matter what." He made her stop. "Look, you do understand that none of this is your fault, right? You did the right things, at least as right as anyone could do with this stupid mess."

"Did you hear Mom? I mean, when she was pounding on my door—" Zoey tried to swallow the lump in her throat. "What she was saying?"

"Yes, I heard, sweetheart," Benjamin said gently.

"I . . ." A sob.

She felt Benjamin put his arms around her again, fumbling at first, finding her in his eternal night.

"I thought I was getting over this," she managed to say. "I thought I was all cried out."

"Not yet," Benjamin said. "Maybe not ever."

My darling—

I've just received your letter. I don't know what to say. I don't know what I can say.

You say you want to keep the baby, fine. I told you I would marry you and raise the baby as my own and give it all the love I can. You know that. You don't have to go back to Jeff just because you're pregnant with his baby. I mean, please, Darla, this is the seventies. We're not our parents, trapped in all kinds of stupid social demands. My parents got married and I don't think there ever was any real love or understanding between them. I've seen what that is like.

All that's really important is that I love you and you love me. And I know you love me, no matter what you say. You can tell me all you want that you have always loved Jeff but I don't believe it. I can't believe it because I'm not going to just go on thinking this was nothing but a temporary fling for you. I don't know what I'd do if I believed that.

What will I do if I don't have you? Do my tour and then move back to Maine alone? I always saw you there with me. Or anywhere, as long as there's you. I know you don't like the army, so maybe I could get an early out. Anything.

Please write me. You can't call for the next week because we'll be out on field maneuvers, but please write. If I see a letter waiting for me when I get back I'll know it's all going to be all right. Please, please don't let it end. Please write.

I know this sounds pathetic and desperate but I don't care anymore.

I love you.

Fred

Nineteen

Nina had awakened in the night, sweating and panting, after one of the nightmares. It was one of the usual, one she'd had many times before, full of dread and shame. They came a little less frequently now, since she had confronted her uncle over his molestation and since she had been seeing the shrink once a week. But they still came.

And yet they had lost a lot of their power. In the past she would never have been able to get back to sleep. And, sleeping, to have dreamed of far more pleasant things so that when the alarm went off, blasting some old Jimi Hendrix near her ear, she awoke a second time, content.

She started to turn off the alarm, then realized that the wailing guitar was certain to annoy Claire, whose room was upstairs. Claire was not a morning person. Neither was Nina, really, but Claire tended to walk around for the first hour of the day in a surly bad mood. And the rest of the day, too.

Nina got up, pulled on a robe, ran to the shower, and found to her annoyance that Claire had beaten her to it. So she headed downstairs.

Her father was at the big antique pine table in the kitchen, wearing his inevitable charcoal gray suit and eating bacon and scrambled eggs. There was a small fire in the kitchen fireplace, and Nina took the chair closest to it. Through the French doors she could see a grubby, gray day that looked like rain.

"Bacon? Eggs? I guess you've stopped worrying about that cholesterol thing, huh?" She grabbed a huge blueberry muffin from the basket and poured herself some coffee.

Her father gave her a guilty look. "I have bran muffins practically every day. Plus, look, I'm having juice." He pointed to the glass of grapefruit juice. "And I hit the gym three times a week. And I lost four pounds. And why am I making excuses to you?"

"Excellent point, Dad," Nina said. "You shouldn't be making excuses to me."

"Then I'll just go ahead and eat this bacon."

"You should be making excuses to someone else. Only there isn't anyone else."

Her father chewed his bacon and looked at her suspiciously.

"You know, Claire and I were talking the other day, and she said that for an old guy you're not bad looking."

"How generous of her," Mr. Geiger grumbled.

"You have nice hair," Nina pointed out. "Although I do have two words for you—Grecian Formula."

"Gray hair is good for bank presidents," he argued. "It makes me look distinguished."

"Like people could feel safe giving you their money."

"Exactly."

"Aha! But who do you give *your* money to?"

Mr. Geiger rolled his eyes. "You know, you could

just try asking, without all the preliminaries. How much do you want?''

''Whatever you have on you, Dad, since you're offering, but that's not really what I was talking about.'' She fixed him with a critical look. ''You need to start dating. Claire is worried you'll end up like one of those old guys who sit on the benches at the mall and stare at people all day. Wearing a little hat and pulling your pants up to your chest and walking in little tiny steps, shuffle, shuffle over to spit in the trash can. All alone in some old people's home where perky volunteers from religious cults come on weekends and force you to play patty-cake and make ceramic ashtrays.''

''Claire said all this?''

''She's just trying to be nice, Daddy,'' Nina said, with every possible appearance of sincerity. ''Besides, I think she's right about you dating. What about when Claire returns to her home planet? What about when I go off to be a professional groupie? You'll be here eating bacon all alone.''

Mr. Geiger nodded reflectively. ''I guess when you're both gone, I'll miss the cheeriness and optimism you bring now. You know, not ten minutes ago I was thinking, well, the bacon is crisp and life is good. Now I'm thinking of drowning myself.''

''I have this teacher—'' Nina said, letting it hang.

''Yes? Does he have something else depressing to add to the conversation?''

''She.''

''Okay, she.''

''No, I mean she's a *she*. Divorced. Twice, I think, but she doesn't have any kids.''

''Oh. Too bad. Kids are such a joy,'' he said dryly.

"Mrs. Bonnard. She teaches English, and she's not bad looking. She has blond hair and she keeps in shape, although I don't think it's real. The hair."

"Let me guess—having trouble with your grades in English?"

"Dad! You're so cynical. Besides, what if she didn't like you? Then my grade could actually go down." Not by much, Nina admitted privately, since it was pretty close to the bottom already.

"I don't think I need any help getting set up," Mr. Geiger said firmly.

"That's what I told Claire," Nina said. "But she said you were getting old and kind of out of it. I said you were just like forty or something, but she kept saying that was pretty old if you were going to meet someone to be with in your old age."

"Claire said that?" he asked sourly.

"I told her you have all kinds of opportunities to meet women at work and you're still young and good looking. But she said, face it, all he really has going for him is that he has money."

"All I have . . . Oh, really? It's nice to know your sister has such a high opinion of me."

"Yeah. Well, anyway, all I was trying to say was that if you ever wanted to go out with someone, it would be okay with me." She smiled kindly. "Claire was the one who thought you needed help."

She got up from the table just as Claire entered the room, looking as annoyingly perfect as always, though her hair was wrapped in a towel.

"I hope you left some hot water," Nina said, grinning hugely.

Claire ignored her. "Good morning, Daddy."

"Oh, good morning, huh?" Mr. Geiger pointed an

accusing finger at Claire. "Sit down, Miss High-and-Mighty. You and I are going to have a little talk."

Zoey and Benjamin left the house together, walking in strained silence down to the ferry. They had already discussed everything that could be discussed. They had considered skipping school but decided it would be smarter just to get out of the house. Even school was better than risking being drawn into the next round of the war between their parents.

Neither their mother nor their father had been at the breakfast table, and Zoey and Benjamin had hurried out early rather than risk an encounter.

As they passed the restaurant, they saw that it was closed. A man was rattling the door, perplexed. He spotted Zoey and Benjamin.

"Hey. How come you're closed?"

Benjamin answered for them. "My folks are a little sick."

"More than a little," Zoey muttered under her breath in an attempt at black humor.

"Hope it's nothing serious," the man called after them.

"Yeah, well, guess again," Benjamin said to Zoey, catching her mood.

"It's going to rain," Zoey said.

"Of course it is," Benjamin said.

"Closed the restaurant," Zoey said wonderingly. Her parents had almost never closed on a normal business day. The last time had been during Benjamin's surgery, when they had shut down for a week.

A thin drizzle began to fall. They stood stoically side by side, both beyond caring about anything as minor as rain.

* * *

Jake had gone for an early morning run after doing his usual stomach crunches and pushups. He'd seen his father at breakfast. Neither of them had mentioned the events of the previous day as they sat at the table being fussed over by Jake's mother. Both he and his father knew that the subject would never be mentioned between them. But they also both knew that there had been a fundamental change in their relationship.

Jake had lived his life with an eye always on pleasing his father. Living up to his father's ideals. Being the son that Wade was supposed to have been, had he lived.

But that was over now. The full impact had not yet sunk in, but that stage of Jake's life was over. Whatever he did from now on would not be about pleasing or impressing his father.

He walked down the steep driveway and along the beach with thoughts slowly turning through his mind. Claire. Wade. Zoey.

A great many things had changed in a very short time. He had made a lot of mistakes. And he had finally learned that he had to forgive the mistakes of others in order to be forgiven himself. So in time he would forgive his father. But nothing would ever turn back the clock for the two of them.

He found Zoey and Benjamin together at the ferry landing, silent and gray in the cold drizzle. He stood near them, saying nothing.

There wasn't a damned thing to say.

Lucas was just leaving his house when he saw Aisha walking down the hill from the bed-and-breakfast. She normally took the little shortcut down to Bristol

Street. He walked rapidly toward her to meet her before she turned off. Maybe she could tell him what was going on with Zoey. First the way she had blown up at him, then the startling explosion of late-night shouting from the Passmore house. It had been loud enough to wake Lucas's parents. His father had been on the verge of calling down to them to shut up, that people had to sleep.

"Hi, Aisha." She looked grim and downcast. Probably the horizon-to-horizon pall of gray cloud.

"Hi, Lucas."

"What's up?"

She shook her head. Nothing.

He fell into step with her. "Hey, Aisha? You don't have to answer this if you don't want to."

"What?"

"What's going on with Zoey? I'm lost here."

"Zoey?" Aisha looked impatient. "What do you mean?"

"I guess nothing."

They walked along, reaching Town Beach, just a hundred paces behind Jake. A light rain had begun. Lucas checked his watch. Ten minutes till the ferry. Hopefully the rain wouldn't fall any harder.

"Lucas?" Aisha said, surprising him.

"Yeah?"

"Lucas, did you tell Christopher how to get a gun?"

Lucas took her arm. "Are you telling me he has one?"

She stared suspiciously at him. Her eyes were red. "Did you help him get it?"

He shook his head. "No. He asked me to, but I said no."

Aisha started walking again. He looked up at the

sky. A little sunshine would have been nice. He'd always believed that nothing really bad could happen to him as long as the sun was shining. This was a day for disaster.

Twenty

Benjamin hated it when the weather drove them onto the lower deck of the ferry. It was overheated and smelled of paint, diesel fumes, and damp wool. The noise of the engines was much louder, blanking out the sounds of the water.

He sat on one of the outer benches, leaning his head back against a cold Plexiglas window. He had been with Zoey, but she had gone to the rest room. Nina took her place, but this morning he didn't even want to be with Nina. Silence was the best refuge from all the emotions of the long night.

"I got Claire so good this morning," Nina said gleefully, without preliminary. "Hey. Your hair's wet, you know."

"I noticed," he said. Not rude, but in such a way that she could have known that he wanted to be left alone. *Would* have known if she'd been the kind of person to read clues, to pay attention to subtleties. Claire would have known.

Something was rubbing on his head.

"What are you doing?" Definitely angry now. Even Nina had to see that.

"I'm drying your hair with my scarf."

"My hair's fine."

"You have wet hair. Why didn't you wear a hat or a hood or something?"

"Look, Nina, my hair is fine, okay? Leave it alone; my hair is fine."

The rubbing stopped. She fell silent. For about thirty seconds.

"So, anyway, I was talking to my dad, telling him he should maybe think about dating—"

Benjamin laughed, a harsh sound.

"That's not the funny part," Nina pointed out.

"It's irony. Perfect irony," he said bitterly.

"It is? Why?"

He waved his hand impatiently. "Forget it. It's a long and pretty sickening story."

"My favorite kind of story. Tell me all about it. It has to be more interesting than the homework I should be doing."

He shook his head. "I don't think so." Claire would have let it drop. But would Nina? No, of course not. She couldn't even tell that he was ready to lash out, that he was barely restraining himself.

"Come on, you have to tell me."

"It's really none of your damn business, Nina," he snapped.

A momentary silence, then, "Tell me anyway."

"Why?" he asked wearily. "I told you to drop it, so why do you insist on pushing it?"

The touch of her hand on his was surprising. "Because it's something really bad," she said softly, her lips so near his ear that he could feel her warm breath. "I can tell it's bad, Benjamin, and you need to tell me."

"You don't want to know." For some reason he felt near to tears. It was amazing. Where had that come from?

"If you tell me, you'll feel better."

Lord, now he really was crying. Good grief, how pathetic. He hadn't broken down all night with Zoey. He'd been strong and dealt with it. Now, with Nina . . .

"I'm sorry," he said, wiping under his shades. "Look, Nina, I don't want to lay all this on you."

"I'm your girlfriend, right? I'm the person you're supposed to tell things to."

He nodded, fighting a fresh wave of tears. "Yeah, you are my girlfriend." Yes, he thought with sudden clarity, yes. Claire would have known to leave him alone when he was snapping and defensive and wanted his privacy. But Nina had known better. She hadn't done what he wanted. She had done what he needed.

"Well, at least we have that straight," Nina said drolly. "I'm the girlfriend, you're the boyfriend. It's the traditional arrangement—one of each."

He smiled. "Yeah. And um, look, Nina?"

"Yes?"

"I love you, Nina."

"I'm really glad, because I love you, too, Benjamin."

Satisfaction in her voice? Yes. And a profound relief in his own heart. He would tell Nina, and then, yes, he would feel better.

"Now spill," Nina ordered. "And don't leave out any of the good stuff."

In the ferry bathroom Zoey threw up. She rinsed her mouth out with ice-cold water from the tiny tap. She found a piece of gum in her purse and chewed it.

Outside, she saw Lucas waiting for her.

"I want to give this one more try," he said, blocking her way.

"What are you talking about?" She still felt sick. Sick and weary enough that if her knees had simply collapsed, she wouldn't have been surprised.

"Us, Zoey," he said. "I want to know what's going on with us."

She shrugged. "I don't know, Lucas."

"Look, Zoey, I still love you."

For some reason this struck her as funny. "You do? Well. That's good. Love is a great thing. But you know, it's about half b.s. Maybe it's more like two-thirds b.s."

"Zoey, what is the matter with you?"

"You know how they say wake up and smell the coffee? I'm smelling it. Is it French roast? That's what it smells like. You wake up, you open your eyes, and hey, guess what? People aren't what you think they are."

"Zoey, are you drunk?"

She shook her head. "Tired is all. Tired of . . . everything."

"Look, come sit down with me. You need to sit down, babe, you're swaying back and forth."

"Oh, man," Zoey said with profound regret. "You seem so nice sometimes."

He smiled the smile that had made her love him. "Sometimes I am nice."

"Yep. Sometimes. Only who knows, right? You might know someone for years and years. Your whole life, maybe. They seem nice. But who really ever knows? How? How can you know for sure?"

Lucas looked worried and confused. "I don't know, Zoey."

Zoey nodded, woozy, disgusted with herself, still

sick to her stomach. Why wouldn't he just go away? She wanted to sit and go to sleep.

"I just need to know one thing, Zoey."

"Uh-huh."

"Do you still love me? If you do, then we can deal with everything else. But I have to know. I have to know if you still love me."

Something like awareness, consciousness, reawoke in Zoey's mind. He was waiting. Inches away. He looked scared and sad and hopeful. If she just said yes, he would let her be. And she did love him, didn't she? Wouldn't she, when this nightmare was over? Wouldn't that same feeling return, despite everything?

"I don't know anymore," she said. "I don't know anything."

Twenty-one

''Morning announcements.'' Mr. Hardcastle's voice, crackling over the ancient intercom system, the background music of homeroom, almost always ignored.

Claire clenched her jaw and, without turning her head, watched Jake move to a vacant seat behind Zoey. He whispered something in her ear and she turned to give him a strange, tortured smile. He squeezed her shoulder and she patted the hand where it lay.

Then he got up and, with what subtlety he could manage at more than six feet and nearly two hundred pounds, moved back to his seat beside Claire.

''Attention, all seniors,'' Mr. Hardcastle went on. ''A reminder that the first round of SATs is coming up very soon. Prep books and number-two pencils are available for sale at the school store.''

A general groan at the mention of SATs. *Good,* Claire thought. She wanted to get the test over with, the sooner the better.

''Hi,'' Jake whispered, looking guilty.

''Was Zoey interviewing you about the drug story just now?'' She said it just a little too loudly to be completely discreet. Jake looked around, horrified, but of course no one was listening; they were all lost in grim contemplation of SATs.

''She's dropping that,'' he whispered back.

''How nice of her,'' Claire said. ''How ever did you convince her?''

Jake shot her a sharp glance.

Good, so her annoyance wasn't going totally unnoticed.

He shrugged. ''I guess she decided it wasn't worth doing.''

''Did she decide this while you were groping her on the football field yesterday?''

The bell rang and the class jumped to its feet.

''You saw that? I mean, it was nothing, Claire,'' Jake said, switching to a more normal speaking voice in the din of scraping chairs and loud chatter.

''I see lots of things, Jake. And what I don't see, I hear about.''

A flash of pure guilt on his guileless face. ''Like what?''

Like what? he asks. *Like what*? Claire sneered. ''You know something, Jake? You should stick to being a big, straight-arrow jock. You're really not cut out for being clever.'' The remark was meant to wound, and Claire could see that it had.

''Claire, with Zoey and me yesterday, that's just something separate. It's . . . not anything like what you think it is.''

''Oh, I know you still keep a little torch burning for Snow White,'' Claire said. ''It's pathetic, but it doesn't lower you in my opinion nearly as much as the other. Louise, Jake? Yes, I know about that, too. Your first time, Jake, and it was stinking drunk with Lay-Down Louise.'' She gave him a contemptuous smile. ''You must be so proud.''

* * *

He would never do it. He would never do it. Aisha had repeated the phrase over and over again, reassuring herself, trying to make herself believe it. Christopher would never do it. Since the night before, the terrifying night before, with Christopher already deeply under the spell of the gun. All through the school day in a trance state, swinging wildly between relief and dread, each swing of the pendulum taking her farther and farther.

He would never do it. Christopher wasn't that kind of person. He would never do it.

She had looked for him at lunch and found him in the storeroom, hunched over, looking at it, scowling like a cat with a dead mouse. A strange, intense light in his eyes.

But still, she told herself, he would never do it.

As soon as the last-period bell rang, she ran to the gym. She would catch him before he left. She would do whatever it took. She would knock him out before she would let him leave with that gun. If that didn't work, she'd tell the principal, even the police. Anything to stop him, although she knew that he would never do it.

And if he did?

What then? Could she turn him in to the police? Why? For doing to the scum just what they'd love to do to him? Would she see him destroyed when all he had wanted was justice?

But if she just let it happen, and then afterward kept quiet . . . then she would be a part of it. There was no greater sin, and she would be part of it. Part of evil. Not justice, the evil of bloodthirsty vengeance.

She arrived, breathless, at the equipment room.

Coach Anders, the girls' gym teacher, was there, stuffing basketballs into a big canvas sack.

"Hey, hey. Now, why can't I get you to run like that in gym?"

"Sorry, Coach Anders." Aisha felt foolish. Of course she was running for nothing. This was all silly. "I was looking for Christopher Shupe."

"Oh, really?" Coach Anders put on a wise, knowing look. "You two, huh? Well, that's all right. Christopher's a good guy. You know he has four jobs? People don't work like that anymore."

That's right, Aisha told herself. *People don't, but Christopher does because Christopher knows where he's going, and what he wants, and he doesn't let anything keep him from his goal of college and a life and a future*. "Um, is he in the back?"

"No, he took off."

Aisha's heart sank. "Off to his next job, I guess," she said brightly.

"He took the van over to pick us up a new volleyball net."

"The—what van?"

"The one we have for the phys-ed department."

Aisha rocked back, almost losing her balance.

"He just left," Coach Anders said. "Said he had a couple errands of his own, so I told him to take his time."

Lucas waited throughout the day for the apology he knew must come from Zoey. But in homeroom she'd only had time for Jake. At lunch, nothing. In history, where they sat near each other, still nothing. Last-period French, nothing. Not so much as a smile. She had torn out his heart and couldn't even be bothered to spare him a simple smile of encouragement.

And yet he didn't believe it was over. Something else was going on. Maybe it was all part of some long, drawn-out punishment for what had happened in Vermont. Maybe she was just trying to tell him never to pressure her again. Or maybe she was just being overly dramatic about the whole thing. If so it was an unattractive part of her personality.

It occurred to him that whatever was troubling her might have something to do with the shouting he'd heard from the Passmore house the night before, but that was no excuse. In his home, hostility and anger were on the daily menu and he didn't take it out on Zoey.

He still believed she would come around. But at the same time he was humiliated about being treated this way, like a bad little boy who had to be punished for the sin of being a normal, heterosexual guy.

It wasn't over with Zoey; *that* he couldn't stand to believe. But the relationship needed an adjustment. Definitely. Zoey needed to be taught that he wasn't kidding when he'd said there were other girls out there in the world. Girls who wouldn't treat him like crap.

All this had been going through his mind as he walked, almost without thinking, from French class down the stairs and through the hall to Claire's locker.

Claire was removing some books from the locker. She had a look that, had he seen it in any other eyes, he would have thought was sadness. Perhaps disappointment.

"Hi, Claire."

"Hi, Lucas."

"So." He stuck his hands in his pockets. "Thinking of going for a drive again?"

* * *

Aisha dropped the key ring on the floor of the car and had to scrabble around to find it. Her hands were shaking so badly that she could barely insert the key, and as she backed her parents' Taurus out of the parking space in the public garage, she nicked the front bumper on one of the concrete support pillars.

She knew the van. It was painted in the school colors. If she could find it, she would recognize it. And after all, Weymouth wasn't such a large town, was it?

Only it had to be before the falling sun disappeared altogether. Already in the cloud-smothered gloom all colors were turning gray, and in the dark she would never find him.

"Silly," she told herself. "He's just acting tough. He's not going to do it."

She drove erratically, jerking to sudden stops when she spotted something like the van. Accelerating away from stoplights only when the impatient horns reminded her to move. She was dizzy from swiveling her head, looking this way and that. With each new street she passed, she was haunted by the possibility that she might have made a wrong decision, driven right past him, missing her chance to save Christopher by a matter of a few feet because of a choice to go left instead of right.

The early commute was starting, filling the streets with cars, slowing her progress, frustrating her decisions. One-way streets. Stoplights. Blocked intersections. A bus that wouldn't move. Horns. Headlights snapping on as the early darkness descended.

There! She stepped on the gas. Was it him? Could she catch him?

A shriek of metal on metal. She'd hit something! A parked car. But there was no time to stop; the van—

was it the right van?—was gaining, taking advantage of a hole in traffic.

No. The van turned, and she saw that it wasn't him.

Somewhere a siren, too loud. Flashing blue lights reflecting in her rearview mirror, distracting her.

"Pull your vehicle to the curb."

The electronically amplified voice surprised her. She realized the police car had been behind her for several blocks. It was her they were after.

She pulled the car to the curb and felt as if she might collapse. Night was falling fast. The police would take their time writing her ticket. It was over. She was too late. She couldn't stop him in time.

Christopher drove the van slowly the length of Brice Street, waiting for darkness.

The gun was on his lap, protected, nestled there. Sometimes he touched it, reassured by the coldness of it and yet disturbed. He had been in a state of nervous excitement all day. It was almost like being high. An exalted, alive feeling. A tingling in the skin and fingers, a buzzing in his head.

Kick me, will they? he repeated in his head, an imaginary conversation. *Kick me? Spit on me? I don't think so. Won't happen again, that's for damned sure. Won't kick anyone, ever again.*

The street ended at the river and he turned around, tires crunching over fallen leaves and the rusted coils of a ruined wire fence.

Back up the street, just a few feet now, creeping as slowly as the van would go.

He leaned across to roll down the passenger-side window. Maybe the bastard would make it easy. Maybe he'd come out to the street or into his front yard. Then he could do it through the window.

Hey, dude? Guess what, man? Remember the guy you were kicking in the balls? Remember that? Remember all the trash you were talking while you did it? You do remember? Good. Now suck on this. Not so tough now, are you?

He passed the house and pulled over to the shoulder of the road, a hundred yards farther down. He couldn't wait for the creep to come out. He couldn't have this drag on forever. The time was now.

He got out of the van, sliding the cold automatic into the waist of his pants, hidden under his jacket. He plunged into the woods as he'd done before, skirting around, the river now close on his left. In the dark he stumbled into a patch of thorns, which tore at his legs, fueling his rage.

He was at a pitch now, pumped, vibrating with impatient energy. Every muscle and sinew tight, eyes wide, nose flared, alive! He'd never been so alive!

The barking of a dog. But not directed at him. No, the dog was barking at the back door of the grubby house. Hungry.

Perfect!

The punk would come out to feed his dog. Any second now . . . yes! The door was opening.

He came out. He was wearing military fatigues and unlaced boots. He was carrying a bag of dog food and an open can.

"Hey, boy," he said, his voice utterly clear to Christopher's hyper-alert senses. "You hungry, boy? Yeah. Come on."

Christopher crept closer. Like a soldier closing in on his enemy. That's what he was—a soldier. Doing an honorable deed in a righteous war that he hadn't started but would damned sure finish.

Twenty-two

Claire drove in a different direction this time. South, toward Portland. For a while neither she nor Lucas said much at all. Claire concentrated on driving and tried not to think about Jake. What Lucas concentrated on, Claire couldn't say, but he was grim and far away for a long time, hunched over, staring out the side window.

At last Claire pulled off onto a side road that dead-ended on a bluff overlooking the sea. She left the engine running, keeping the heat on.

She turned sideways on the seat. "Are you going to tell me why we're taking this drive?" she asked. "You didn't seem to enjoy the one the other day."

"Things change," Lucas said.

"Do they?"

He looked at her. The dark eyes had changed over the years, grown more wary, perhaps. Yet they were the eyes he had once looked into with something like love.

"Sometimes they change so much you feel like you've come full circle and back to a place you've been before," he said.

So. That's what this was about. She was a little surprised. Even a little disappointed in Lucas. "Full circle back to a beach a long time ago?'' Claire asked, knowing the answer.

He nodded. ''Back to a first kiss.''

She should put an end to this. She really should. But the memories were strong for her, too. There had been a time when she would have done anything for Lucas Cabral. And it would be a down payment on paying Jake back. ''Are you going to ask me as politely as you did then, Lucas, with your voice all squeaky and trembling?'' she said, half-mocking, half-trembling with anticipation.

Lucas slid toward her, closer, close enough that the slightest movement would bring them together. ''Do I have to ask?''

''No,'' Claire said. ''You don't.''

Christopher stood, drew up the gun, pointed it straight at the boy as the boy tossed the empty dog food can into the trash barrel.

''Don't move,'' he said.

The boy jerked and stared wildly.

''Don't move,'' Christopher repeated in a silky, dangerous voice.

''What do you want, man? What's going on? What is this?'' Eyes wide, throat swallowing convulsively. Fear. Raw, stomach-churning fear.

''Remember me?'' Christopher asked, grinning. He had moved closer. The gun was pointed right at that shaved head. Right at that sickly little mustache and goatee.

''No man, look, what is this, man? I don't have any money or anything. Honest to God, whatever you want you can have it, but look, don't shoot me. Don't shoot me, man.''

''I'm the guy you were calling nigger,'' Christopher said, his voice rising, feeding off the fear.

"I don't know . . . just don't shoot me." Placating hands held up.

"You and your punk-ass skinhead piece of crap friends *kicked* me."

Was that a faint, dawning comprehension in those terrified eyes? Was the fear growing still deeper? Good. Good, let it grow. Christopher felt an urge to laugh out loud. The rush of power! Absolute power! He clicked off the safety. The skinhead knew what he had done. A dark stain was growing down the front of his fatigue trousers. There was the smell of urine and sweat.

"Look man, look man, no, look, don't man. Don't shoot me, man."

He was begging. Praying to Christopher like he was some kind of a god. And with his gun, with his finger on the trigger, with the slightest pressure now, the difference between life and death, *wasn't* he like a god?

From far away the sound of a siren floated through the trees. The dog had started barking, jerking frantically at its chain. The skinhead had sunk to his knees, crying.

And the gun felt so powerful in Christopher's hand.

Zoey's parents were waiting in the living room when she and Benjamin arrived home. Her mother sitting, staring blankly, eyes red, skin pale. Older than she had ever looked.

Her father was pacing back and forth, biting savagely at a thumbnail. When Zoey and Benjamin came in, their father looked up sharply.

It was a moment of frozen time. No one said anything. No one moved.

Then her mother broke the spell. "Both of you sit down, please." A colorless voice.

Zoey sat stiffly. Benjamin found the easy chair across from her after some fumbling. They rarely used the living room, spending most of their time in the family room.

"We, um . . . we have something to tell you," Mr. Passmore said. He sighed shakily. "It looks like your mother and I will be separating."

Benjamin hung his head.

"A lot of bad things have been said and done around here lately," Mr. Passmore went on.

"I'm so sorry, Zoey," her mother interrupted. "Yelling at you like that . . . blaming *you.* I don't know how to tell you how desperately sorry I am."

Zoey bit her lip. "That's not what you need to be sorry for," she managed, in a grating, unnatural voice.

"Look, let's—" Her father raised a quieting hand, struggling to maintain calm. "Let's not make this any worse than it has to be. We've decided maybe we need some time apart. We're going to keep the restaurant going, at least for now, but I'm going to move out. Find a place . . ."

Zoey jumped up, rushing to his side. She threw her arms around him, holding him tightly. "Why should you move out, Daddy? It was her, not you."

"Zoey," Benjamin said, cautioning her, but without much conviction.

"This is your fault," Zoey said, directing a look of pure hatred at her mother. "You did this." Her mother blanched and recoiled. Her father pushed her away gently, holding her at arm's length.

"No, Zoey," he said. "I know what you saw. But that's not all of it. As much as I love you I can't have you thinking your mother was the only one in the wrong.''

''Don't defend her!'' Zoey cried in outrage. ''She's destroying this family.''

''No, Zoey. It's not that simple.'' He turned away and seemed to be struggling to gain control of himself. Zoey stood helpless, her arms at her sides, not knowing where to turn or what to do.

''This all goes back a long time,'' Mr. Passmore said at last. ''You were asking the other night about when we first got together. I told you there had been another man in your mother's life. Well, I didn't know until . . . you know . . . but it was—well, I guess you know who it was.''

''There was nothing between Fred McRoyan and me, not since we were married,'' her mother said fiercely. ''We had put it all behind us. It was over.'' She shot a furious look at her husband.

Mr. Passmore nodded. ''I accept that, Darla. I do.''

''Not until I found out—''

''Let's not do this again,'' Mr. Passmore said. ''I don't ever want to fight in front of the kids again. This is wrong.'' He took a deep breath. ''There's something you kids don't know. While I was in Europe, backpacking around, while your mom was seeing . . . Fred . . . anyway, I also met a girl. An American girl who was traveling like me. We had an affair.''

Zoey sank back onto the couch.

''And—and since then, I've seen her again. She lives down in Portland, and your mother, well, found out that I had seen this woman several times since we've been married. That's why she . . . well, you were getting back at me, right?'' He directed this last question to his wife, putting on a bitterly cheerful tone. "And did an excellent job of it."

Zoey saw her mother's eyes were full of tears. She realized her own were, too. This was it—the destruction of her family. The end. Even more, the destruction of her parents, all their tawdry, humiliating secrets now laid out to sicken their children. Zoey wished she could just disappear. If she'd still had even an ounce of energy or will, she might have grabbed Benjamin's hand and run. But all she could do was watch and listen, helpless to change anything.

"You might as well tell them the rest," Zoey's mother said flatly.

Mr. Passmore nodded. "Yes. The rest. It seems while I was with this woman in Europe, well, it seems she became pregnant."

Zoey felt the world spinning around her.

"See, you both, Zoey, Benjamin, you have . . . a sister."

Making Out: Lucas Gets Hurt

Betrayal. Mistakes. Past Loves. What else could it be but book 7?

Zoey's parents broke up and it rocked her world. Then **Lucas** watched miserably as **Zoey** was comforted by her old boyfriend, **Jake.** Now **Lucas** tries to hold off **Claire,** his old love, who says she'll do anything to get **Lucas** back. Whatever happens. . .

Lucas Gets Hurt.